Trinity

c.j. bolyne

Cluster Publishing

Trinity

C.J. Bolyne

Amazon Edition

Published by Cluster Publishing

For information, address Cluster Publishing, 127 Home Street N., Steinbach, Manitoba R5G 2B2

ISBN 13: 978-0-9879625-0-8

ISBN 10: 0987962507

ISBN: Ebook - 978-0-9879625-1-5

Cover design sketch by Madison Hildebrandt

Acknowledgments

To my family who's belief in me gave me the courage to realize a dream.

Thank You.

Hi Boe!

Hope you enjoy

Trinity

C J Bolyne

Introduction

In our world, there are gods. Many gods of many lands. Each land had their own realm of gods.

For millennia, the realms and all the lands lived in peace with each other.

The kingdom of Gwynneth's gods were split into two factions; The Guardians, who wished nothing but peace and prosperity among humanity, and The Anord, who wished only misery and despair. For all the good done, there was the equivalent of evil done. This was the balance of life, amongst the gods and humanity alike.

The Anords of Gwynneth, however, grew weary of this existence. They wanted more. They wanted to rule all gods and all of humanity. Their greed and lust for power grew until the Guardians had no choice but to meet them on the battlefield of Trinity. The order of things had to be restored. The battle was fierce. It raged for days.

Near the end, Liesson, God of combat and honour, was in a fatal battle with Koris, god of winter and cold.

Koris fell before Liesson. Seconds later, a horrible scream was heard by all the gods. So horrible, they came to an instant halt. All eyes fell on the god who produced this scream.

Payton. Young goddess, daughter of Liesson and Ardaria.

The battle ended … for now.

Chapter 1

Damn! Damn! Damn! She thought to herself. Concentrate girl! It wasn't that good. Or was it?

Payton stood looking in the mirror. Just staring at herself. 'Gotta get ready for work.' She had a hard time putting her eye liner on. The stranger she helped the night before had her stomach in knots. He just popped out of nowhere while she was digging for her keys in front of her apartment block. His face bloody, clothes torn, and he could hardly walk. He scared the crap out of her!

"Help .... Please" he whispered. Then he collapsed.

Payton helped him to his wobbly feet and into her apartment. Tried to lay him on her sofa gently but her arm slipped and he fell on it with a thud. His moan made her wince. "Sorry" she said. 'What the hell am I doing?' she yelled in her head. 'Some street bum asks for help and you let him in your home? For all you know, he's a nut case!'

She looked down at him. 'What happened to you?' she thought. 'Never mind – I don't think I want to know. Let's get you cleaned up. No, wait. I should call for an ambulance.' She reached for the phone on the coffee table, when his hand grabbed hers. "No, don't!" he said. "I'll be okay." "But you need help!"

Payton protested. “No … you can’t” he said, starting to pull himself up, slowly.

She could see the pain he was in. “Can I get you anything?” she asked.

“No, thank-you. May I use your washroom to clean-up a bit?”

“Uh, yeah … yeah.” She replied. “It’s this way.”

Helping him to his feet was no easy task. He was tall and built – well built, she could feel his muscles under his torn t-shirt. Kind of heavy for her 5’6” frame to hold up. She helped him to the washroom, sitting him on the edge of the bathtub.

“Thank-you,” he said “I’ll be out in a while.”

“Okay.” she hesitated, then shut the door.

She went back to her front door to lock it and then to her living room to wait, fingers tapping on the coffee table. ‘What’s taking him so long?’ Thirty minutes had gone by. ‘Maybe I should check on him.’ Just as she rose to head for the washroom, the door opened up. The stranger walked out quietly, calm and looked no worse for wear. ‘Wow!’ she thought as she stared. Clothes were clean, not a scratch on him! “I just needed a little time to re-generate.” He said with a slight grin. ‘No kidding.’ She thought, still staring. This guy was your typical “Adonis” type. Tall, dark, slightly longer hair and dark, almost black eyes. Rugged features and muscles – god – would you look at that! He looks like a god!

“Hello?” he said. His voice snapped Payton back to reality.

"Uh, sorry for staring, but with the shape you were in when I brought you in … and now. How'd you do that? Never mind. Not sure I want to know." Actually, she did want to know, just didn't want to interrogate a stranger. She didn't know who this guy was or what he was capable of.

His dark eyes stared at her; the slight smile on his lips did not fade. "It's okay." he said. "I thank you for your help. I'll let myself out." He started for the door. "Wait!" Payton shouted. He turned. "Are you sure you're alright? I mean. No offense, but you looked terrible just 30 minutes ago … and now … it's like nothing happened!" she stuttered a bit. "How …?"

"You need not concern yourself with that Payton," he said quietly. His voice was quite soothing, soft, his stare gave her shivers.

He walked slowly toward her, leaned down and softly kissed her lips, turned and walked out her front door.

He kissed me! A kiss – what … hey!

How the hell did he know my name?

Sleep that night? Not bloody likely. Payton tossed and turned all night long. When her alarm went off, she slammed her hand down on it, hard. Almost broke the clock – again! She wasn't in good spirits when she had no sleep. Coffee. Coffee was a good thing. 'Get up and move your butt!' talking to herself. Coffee was still steaming on the vanity of the washroom as she finished her hair and make-up. "Presentable" she said, looking at the reflection in the mirror.

Payton never realized how beautiful she really was. If anyone gave her a compliment, she'd smile and say thank-you, but in her thoughts, she'd always think of so many more women in this world more beautiful. Then forget about the whole thing and move on.

Walking to her car that morning was no different than any other morning. It was a nice sunny day, warm, inviting. The kind she wanted to spend outside, go to the beach, maybe the park. Not inside her shop doing someone's hair and listening to local gossip, or listening to the woes of her clients, while doing the latest highlight technique found in this season's hairstyle guide.

Chapter 2

"Morning all!" Payton greeted her staff the same way every day.

"Hey boss!" Ginger sang. 'Just a little too chipper for me!' Payton thought. Ginger seemed to always be in a good mood. She was a petite, pretty, bleach blond, and with the latest cut, always. She'd bop around the shop on a permanent sugar high. At least that is what it looked like.

"Coffee's ready Payton!" Olivia said. "Thanks! I could use more." Payton replied. "Rough night, boss lady?" Teri asked while heading for the coffee pot. Teri was always concerned about everyone. She wore her heart on her sleeve, constantly. She had a classical beauty to her. Tall, slim, dark shoulder length hair: poker straight. High cheek bones, almond shaped hazel eyes and very full lips. Payton wondered if she didn't have collagen injected in her lips, but didn't want to ask. She didn't want to be rude or too nosey.

"So, who's the guy? Oooh, so hot!" Olivia said rather enthusiastically.

"What guy?" Payton replied.

"Geez. I thought you would have bumped into him in the parking lot. He was just in. He asked for an appointment with you – your last one of the day. So I booked it. I'm so jealous. He could warm me up anytime honey! Wow!" Olivia was quite excited about this and it wasn't even her client!

Payton rushed over to the appointment book to see whose name was written in. "Me" was all it said. No name, no phone number.

"He said you'd know who it was." Olivia said, her bright green eyes even bigger than usual. "So, who is he? How'd you meet?"

"Uhggg…when I get my head straight, maybe I'll tell you. Until then, I'll be in my office. Call me when my first client comes in. Thanks Olivia!" Payton said. She went to her office, closed the door, and sat at her desk. 'Look at all this paper. Too many bills!' She sifted through the mail—more bills. Then she saw the note stuck between two bills.

JUST WANTED TO SAY
THANK YOU AGAIN.
WE NEED TO TALK.
WILL SEE YOU LATER

No signature. Great! I help a guy out and he doesn't even tell me his name. We'll see what happens later.

Chapter 3

5:30PM was coming up and still no sign of the stranger. Most clients showed up a few minutes early. Payton was getting anxious. If he didn't show up soon, she'd lock up. Soon, she'd lock up for the weekend. She sent the girls home early. They had no more appointments booked. Olivia was disappointed. She wanted to see 'the guy' again. Payton just gave Olivia a big smile and said "have a good weekend!" as she shut the door behind Olivia.

5:45PM. Still no sign of him. 'Fine,' she thought. She locked the front door, drew the blinds and turned off the lights with the exception of the front window lights. She turned on her heels and stopped short. Staring at her not three feet away was the stranger. Payton's mouth fell open.

"Hello" he said quietly. That slight grin was back on his lips.

"Uh, hey. How'd you get in here? I locked the back door already."

"I have my ways" he answered.

"Yeah, well, that's not an answer to my question. I have a few questions in fact. Like, number one, who are you? And number two, how did you know my name. That's just for starters!" Payton's voice squeaked a little. She was scared now.

The stranger took a step toward Payton. She took a step back. "Stop right there buddy! I do know how to defend myself!" Payton warned. The stranger could see that she was shaking. 'She's terrified of you,' he thought. 'We can't have that. I must calm her; ease her mind.'

"Please, do not be afraid," he tried to use a soothing tone. "I am not here to harm you. I am here to protect you."

"Protect me? From who or what?" Payton demanded.

"It's a long story Payton. I am your guardian. I am Terran." he said.

"Alright, so now I know your name at least. So Terran, who are you and why would I need protection?" she asked.

"Can we go somewhere private to talk?" he asked.

"We are alone here! Right here! So talk!" she started to yell.

"No, we're not" he said and grabbed her around the waist tight. Just before they seemed to disappear from her shop, she saw a shadow figure coming towards her … then darkness.

They landed, or he landed and had to steady her when her knees buckled. She shook her head. It felt fuzzy. When things cleared, she looked around. It was dark, cold and clammy – a cave.

"Where are we?" she asked.

"Safe, for now." he replied.

Terran walked slowly around the cave chanting quietly. Then he stood in the middle of the cave floor, raised his arms, and his hands glowed. 'He GLOWS!' Payton stared at him in total awe.

Terran clapped his hands together hard. The sound was as loud as thunder, or an explosion. She didn't know what it was. She clamped her hands over her ears. It hurt! Then quiet.

When she looked up, Terran was facing her. She looked into those deep eyes – he was so close. She could feel him. She hadn't realized his arms were wrapped around her waist again.

"How I've missed you Payton! So much." He whispered. He kissed her, hard at first. Then soft, oh so soft. Payton felt herself starting to melt in his arms. Suddenly she pushed Terran away as hard as she could.

"What are you doing? I don't even know you!" she said.

"Ah, but you do, my love, you do. I need to help you remember" he replied.

"Remember? Remember what?" she asked.

"Who you are, who you were, your past."

Chapter 4

Payton was in a daze, thinking of the kiss and when Terran cupped her face.

"Payton. Hear me." He began. "I am one of many in an order we call the Guardians. I am what you would call a hybrid; half warlock, half god. We watch over all innocents, such as you. However, you are special."

"Why am I 'special'?" she asked. "There are billions of people in this world and I'm the special one? Come on! You've got to do better than that! This is quite the fairy tale. Once upon a time, there was a beautiful princess…….."

"My task," Terran interrupted, "is to help you regain your memory. We took it and replaced it with a false one when we put you in hiding. Now it is time for you to come back to us, to me." Terran explained. "Many … many years ago, you were a part of the family of Guardians. You are our leader's daughter. In time, you will replace your father and lead us. When the dark warriors found out about you, they made it their mission to destroy you before you took command. You are more powerful than all of us. Even more powerful than your father. Someone like you comes along only once …" Terran drifted off, his gaze on the floor. "And …" Payton snapped. "Huh, … oh forgive me," he said "your memory must be brought back slowly. To bring it back too quickly would cause you too much pain." Terran stopped. He wished he could compel her to remember all. He wanted her to know him again. He was hoping that when he kissed her, there would be a spark of recognition. But, nothing yet.

"How can I really believe such a ridiculous story? You're telling me I'm half warlock and half a god? That's nuts! Besides, I thought women could only be witches or something. Shouldn't I have some 'powers' or something?" Payton started waving her hands in the air ranting. "You show up out of the blue, I take you in, you disappear, and then you show up again and…" Terran grabbed her shoulders and pulled her towards him. His lips met hers with force. That shut her up, he thought as his kiss softened and moved along her cheek to her earlobe. His arms wrapped around her tight. He nibbled her lobe and whispered softly in her ear. Payton froze. Her eyes closed, she started to shake. There were flashes of light in her mind, a flash of her parents, then Terran. She pushed Terran away. Starring at him, she gasped "I know you, from somewhere … but where …" now she drifted.

"Do not try too hard Payton. It will pain you too much." He begged.

"But, I am yours?" she questioned.

"Yes, and I was yours – am yours," he corrected himself.

"I feel you … in my heart, m…my soul, deep within. How can this be? I thought I had a pretty normal life. It's been turned upside down in an instant!" Her baby blues started to tear up. "I don't understand" she cried.

Terran couldn't stand it. He held her trying to comfort her.

"You will know all soon enough, love." He whispered. "Please calm yourself ." She let him hold her, started to relax some. She moved closer resting her head on his chest. She could feel his heartbeat slow and steady. He was warm, inviting. Terran tilted her chin up; he needed to touch those lips again. Those beautiful rosy soft lips. He kissed her gently.

Payton couldn't resist now. She wrapped her arms around his neck. I must be closer, she thought.

Chapter 5

Payton woke up hours later. Eyes half open, she slowly scanned the room. Bedroom! Wait a minute. She sat up, rubbed her eyes again. Looking more closely now. This was not the cave anymore. The walls around the bedroom were stone, perfectly aligned to fit each other. The windows were arched to a point on top. The room was sparsely furnished, with a dresser against the stone wall directly across from the bed. There was another small bureau to her right and two small nightstands on her side of the bed. There were two windows with navy blue curtains that looked like they had seen better days. And a few small paintings on the walls. All looked like they were heavenly beings. This is definitely a man's room, she thought. It could use a woman's touch. Or at least, an interior decorator! One more scan of the walls and her gaze froze on a large portrait behind her. Blankets still wrapped around her, she scrambled to the foot of the bed and stared up. The eyes looking back at her were her own! It was her! The long blond wavy hair, the big baby blues, the rosy lips, that peaches and cream skin. She always thought she'd been lucky to be blessed with such nice skin. Her best feature, she thought. In the portrait, she was wearing a long flowing gown, white. The material criss-crossed the breast and tied behind the neck. A gold braided belt cinched at the waist. Around her neck was a pendant, round, gold, with strange symbols she'd never seen. There were so many symbols on the outer rim of the pendant, she couldn't make them out. There were two larger ones in the center – those she could see – with three lines on top of the sword. 'Wonder what that means?' she thought.

Payton sat on the bed staring up at herself, her mind wandering. She didn't hear the bedroom door open.

"Ahem," Terran cleared his throat, "Morning."

She jumped so high, if she'd had claws like a cat, she'd be on the ceiling hanging on for dear life.

'Hmmm. Agility and strength returning. A little on edge though,' he thought.

Payton landed on the bed on all fours. Her eyes were wide and wild, darting around the room till they landed on him. Then a brief moment of fire.

"Whoa, slow down my love. Remember me?"

"You scared the hell out of me!" she shouted. The wicked grin returned to his lips.

"But then, you always enjoyed trying to catch me off guard." She quipped trying not to smile at what just happened. Wait, how did I know that? Not succeeding, her smile faded. How did she manage to jump so high and yet land so easily? Need to know more, much more. Where do I start?

Chapter 6

"I have to get home. I have book work to do, order supplies, etc." she was flustered, confused. "I … I …. I have to go" she stuttered. "You won't get very far," Terran replied. "This fortress is protected, you can't leave. Not yet. Besides, you're a long way from 'home' or what you thought was home."

"What do you mean? I can't go home? I have a life! It may not be extraordinary to you or anyone else, but it is my life none the less!" Payton's anger was growing.

"Please calm down Payton, please," said Terran. "I will explain." He sat down on the bed next to her.

"I'll start with a question. Do you remember the word I whispered in your ear last night?" Payton nodded yes, then asked "What does it mean, '*trocaire*'?"

"It is an old kingdom word meaning Mercy." He answered. Her gaze was still on him, albeit, confused. "It is the first word I needed to use to begin your recall process. When I said the word, what did you see?"

"My parents," she replied "or I think they were and … you. That's it." "They are your parents Payton. Their names are Ardaria and Liesson." He said. "And you know my name, of course, much more too." A slight smile on his lips again. Payton tried to interrupt but Terran cut her off, “I will tell you more, listen.”

He began.

“The life you know now was placed there with the help of all the gods of the order, the Guardians. Even if you tried to go back to your shop, no one will know who you are by now. They never even met you. That life is gone. As for you and I; we are bound together. That is why last night felt familiar to you. Yes, I knew what you were feeling,” he said before she could ask. He continued, “There was a flash and pain too ….” She nodded. “That is why we have to bring your memories back slowly, so as to minimize the pain. Payton, you are a goddess, a most powerful one I might add. In time, your power will come back, slowly. You had a small demonstration a few minutes ago. Anyway,” he sighed, “unfortunately, I can only tell you about some of the things you recall. When you have the flashes and pain, you must tell me what you see. Will you?”

She nodded yes.

“And finally, I must tell you that the ‘gods of chaos’ are seeking you with a vengeance. That’s why you must be protected. The Guardians call them The Anord.”

“They need you. You have power they need. More power than you know. They cannot take your power if you don’t know what it is. They can only try to steal it once you get your full memory. Do you understand?”

“Yes, some … I think.” She said.

“You said I was a goddess. I thought I was part warlock, as you put it.”

“Ah, yes.” He said. “Well, some gods bound with witches and some goddesses bound with warlocks. Not all though. Your parents are both gods.”

“But, you?” she asked.

“My father, a warlock and my mother, a goddess. My father’s name is Aronon and my mother’s, Elrani.” He answered. “But that is enough for now. Please eat some breakfast. You must keep your strength up. When you’re finished, you can take a shower. There are clean clothes for you in the bureau over there.” He was pointing at the small bureau she’d noticed earlier. “I will leave you to your thoughts for a while. You probably want to be alone to absorb what I’ve just told you. I won’t be long though. If you need me, just think of me and I will be here.” With those final words, Terran gently kissed her, turned and left the bedroom.

Payton sat on the bed staring at the tray of food Terran brought in. It held toast, fruit cup which included green grapes, small strawberries, blueberries and cubes of honeydew melon. Four strips of crisp bacon, two eggs – poached – coffee with cream and sugar on the side, plus a glass of orange juice. ‘I’m supposed to eat all of this?’ she thought. After the story she just heard, her mind was jumping from one thing to another. Her parents. She thought they were back in Florida, enjoying their early retirement. Thought she owned her own business, had a place of her own, friends. All fabricated.

Her parents were actually gods! Real gods! There's more than one? Gods of what? Am I an only child? Maybe she had brothers and sisters in the same predicament as her. If that were true, she hoped they were safe. Hoped the Guardians were protecting them too. Then there was Terran. She felt a bond with him like she had with no one else. But it felt right. She could feel fire rising up in her just thinking about it. She closed her eyes for a few seconds to savour the thought.

Thunder rumbled outside the window. Great! Storm coming, she thought. She just finished her shower and was getting dressed. The clothes Terran left for her fit perfectly. How did he know? Yea, right, 'we are bound,' he says. Guess he'd know what size she was. She walked to the window. The sky was growing dark. Lightning flashes in the distance. Looks like it'll be a big one.

Chapter 7

Terran burst through the door! “Gotta go! NOW!” he shouted.

Payton jumped, “Must you do that? Jeez!”

“Come on!” he shouted. He grabbed her arm, pulling her close to him. She could feel that hard body again. Darkness.

She looked up, Terran’s arm still around her waist. Scanning the surroundings, she saw old temples, hieroglyphics, and beautiful sculptures from thousands of years ago. Karnak! She recognized it from the shows she watched on TV! She loved those shows; found she had a real interest, passion if you will, in ancient history. Pulling away from Terran she walked over to one wall of carvings of Pharaoh Seti I. She ran her hands along the wall feeling every crevasse and bump stopping at the cartouche of the famous Pharaoh’s name. “Seti the first. I knew him well.” She whispered. Suddenly her body shook and a flash of bright light: she saw herself and Terran sitting at a dinner table with Seti I, talking and laughing. Just as quickly, the vision was gone. Payton’s knees buckled and she fell to the ground. Terran cursed himself for not being more aware or quick enough to catch her. He reached down and gently lifted her into his arms. She was still a little dizzy. He found a stone slab nearby, walked over and laid her down, being careful not to let her bump her head. "Payton … Payton, are you okay?" she heard him ask. "Yeah, yeah, uh … I'm good." She replied trying to prop herself up on her elbows. She was still a little weak. She lay down again and closed her eyes. "Give me a sec."

"You had a flash again didn't you?" he questioned.

"Yes."

"You must tell me what you saw," he urged.

"Uh, one thing first," she said, now feeling strong enough to sit up.

"Just how old am I?"

"You may not want to know that, my love, at least, not in the 'number' sense." He answered. "Now, tell me what you saw."

"So strange … when I touched the cartouche of Seti I, I saw him, you, and me sitting down at the dinner table. We ate dinner with Seti I. It seemed so real. I could reach out and touch him! Did I know him? I mean, you said my memory would come back slowly, is that part of it?" she asked him, almost hoping it was a fantasy in her head. Not a real memory. What woman would want to know she was several thousands of years old?

"Yes, my love. It was real. We did dine with Seti I. Actually, quite a fascinating man too. He was the richest pharaoh ever and his conquests …"

"Hey!" she interrupted. "Over here."

"Sorry, my love." he said and reached out to take her hands in his. "We did dine with him. After we were bound – today they call it married – we went to Egypt for our honeymoon. Yeah, that's what they call it now, right?"

Payton nodded.

"You always loved Egypt from the time you were a child. So I took you there. Seti I, not being able to attend our wedding insisted on dining with us and throwing us a celebration." He told her.

"Okay," she said. "We're married … uh … bound?" Terran nodded.

"We were friends with the Pharaohs of Egypt?"

Terran nodded.

"So I'm four or five thousand years old?"

Terran nodded again.

Tears started to well up in her eyes. She couldn't believe it. If the few memories she'd recalled were true, there was so much more to come. How could she just forget the history of the world? Forget her family, her own husband! Tears were trickling down her cheeks. Terran walked to her and pulled her close, his arms around her. "I know it is hard for you, my love," he soothed, "we must give it time. You will remember everything in time."

Her tears slowed and she looked up at him. He brought his hands up to her cheeks and gently brushed the tears away. A warm smile on his face, she mustered a faint smile on her own.

Hand-in-hand, they walked the temple, Payton familiarizing herself once again with the great temple.

She stopped and turned to face Terran. "Why did you bring me here?" she asked.

"To get away from Orkat and I thought you'd be happy to see Egypt again." He replied.

"Orkat … who's Orkat?"

"Anord. Somehow he found you and was coming for you. We had to leave fast. This was the first place I thought of." He said. "Oh, yeah and he's the god of storms and lightening. Not a pleasant being!"

"He would've killed me." she said in an almost inaudible tone.

"No, he can't," Terran said. "He wanted the 'honor' of capturing you. He would be a hero in the eyes of his fellow Anord."

"So the storm I saw was actually Orkat, not just your average storm." She said, more a statement than a question.

Terran looked around, scanning the horizon. The day had gone by so fast. Red, orange and yellow shadows were still fighting to keep their place in the clear sky. A noble, but futile quest as the sun was going to set and the night sky would light up with the twinkling of the stars. It will be a beautiful evening. He hoped a peaceful one.

Chapter 8

She awoke with a start. Darkness. Total darkness. Trying to adjust her eyes didn't work. This can't be 'jumping.' She decided to call it 'jumping' when she and Terran disappeared into thin air. Jumping doesn't last this long. It takes only a split second. "Terran" she called into the darkness. "Terran!" she was louder now. "Right here my love" he appeared out of thin air. The room now lit up with a soft glow of candles all around. Payton's eyes scanned the walls, such beautiful paintings and hieroglyphics. Shining gold statues, they gleamed in the candlelight.

"Where are we?" she asked, her eyes fixed on the beautiful portrait of a queen.

"Cleo's place," he replied.

"Cleo's? You don't mean Cleopatra!?! But she's dead!"

"Aw yes. Unfortunate. Let me clarify. This is her tomb, one of the rooms, not her resting place. She's 'resting' in the room beside this one." His tone was a sad one. "She could have been so much more, done so much more. She got greedy."

"So why here? And when was her tomb found?" Payton was full of questions.

"The modern world has not discovered this tomb yet." He continued. "Humanity doesn't know that Octavian had her killed.

People think she committed suicide, although there are those who are suspicious of that story. Anyway, some of her guards managed to sneak her body into this tomb. Perform their rituals in secret. Octavian and his men tried, in vain, to find her but failed. He went back to Rome with the lie of her suicide and reported that he'd had her body cremated, fool that he was. Cleo was the one that humans remember.

"Okay, so are we safe here?" she asked.

"For now." He responded.

"How do the Anords manage to find us? I mean, we jump here and there. It must be hard to keep up." She said.

"They have their spies all around, as do we." He said as he crouched down, eyes darting side to side. "They may be watching us now!" The smirk on his face grew into a large smile. Payton's shocked look relaxed.

"Stop it!" she giggled.

Laughing! He was glad to see a smile on her beautiful face. He rose. Two quick strides and he was at her bedside. He made sure there would always be a bed for her to rest on at night. Not some cold, hard ground. Not for a goddess.

She looked up at him. Those eyes always made him melt.

Chapter 9

"We'd better go now. It's always good to keep moving." Terran said.

Payton crawled out of bed, looked around. Clothes. She needed clothes. Just the thought of clothes and she was dressed in her favorite jeans and pale pink t-shirt with leather sandals on and a cotton jacket over her left arm. She looked at Terran with large eyes and a smile across her face.

"That is fast! You seem to know exactly what I'm thinking!"

"Ah, my love," he said looking at her with those dark eyes, "that was not me; that was you! I see some of your power begins to return!"

"Me? Holy crap, this is sweet! Can't wait to recall more!" she exclaimed.

He motioned for her to slow down. "All in time. Come, we must go!"

She walked over to him; he put his arms around her waist, and darkness.

The sun was bright, hot. The Valley of the Kings. Terran explained that they couldn't use the tomb entrance. That would reveal the tomb to the modern world. She was not due to be found yet. That too, would come in time. One more jump.

Darkness. Then light. We were in the fortress bedroom again. Man, you do need a decorator!

Terran led her out of the bedroom and down a long winding staircase. More stone walls, she thought. Finally at the bottom, she scanned the large foyer. Furnishings were very sparse here too. Not even an area rug – just cold stone floor.

Terran noticed her critiquing the 'décor' and broke the silence.

"We did not have time to decorate when we came here. Things started happening and we had to leave to meet with the rest of The Guardians …" Terran broke off the explanation standing completely still, listening.

"I'm sorry love. I must do this now." That said, he grabbed Payton by the wrist, pulled her close, bent down and whispered in her ear "*Cneasaigh*."

Flash! Her body continued shaking for a few seconds. This time, Terran held her close and waited for the shaking to subside. She would not fall this time.

Weak, she pulled herself away from him. "I saw a fight, uh, battle. The great hall was overrun by Anords and their followers. The Guardians were surprised by the attack. It never happened before … once all comrades; now pitted against each other." She finished, for now.

"The battle you describe took place five days before they sent you away." He said. The sky outside turning dark, they could hear thunder in the distance when suddenly Terran cried out in pain and fell to his knees in front of her. She bent down to see what was wrong. She saw motion out of the corner of her eye. She looked up. Orkat . She didn't know how, but she recognized him.

Payton glanced down and saw that Terran's shoulder was smoldering. He was already getting back on his feet. Her attention went back to Orkat. He was a menacing figure. He stood at least 6'6", body builder physique; she didn't care for that much muscle. Bald head, beady brown eyes, lightning bolt tattoo high on his right cheek bone. Typical, she thought. He's in a toga, except this one is black. Now can you tell which side he's on lassie?

She turned her attention back to Terran. His shoulder no longer smoldering, almost healed.

A loud roar erupted from Orkat, "You really think you can protect her Terran?" Thunder erupted; a flash and lightning bolt appear in both hands. He lifted one arm high, and with a roar, threw the bolt at Terran. Terran leapt out of the way, the bolt hitting the stone was, a deep crevasse – and the smell of burning coal in its wake. Payton stood staring in shock at Orkat. Terran, in a flash, was behind Orkat's left shoulder. He grabbed Orkat and spun him around with all his strength, smashing his fist into Orkat's nose. The air filled with a scream of pain, as he fell to his knees. But, not for long. Orkat jumped up, grabbed Terran, picked him up and tossed him against the stone wall behind Payton. She screamed. "Terran! Terran" She ran over to his limp body on the floor, knelt down and tried to shake him awake. Orkat smiled, looking down on what he thought was a pathetic scene.

"You will come with me!" he demanded.

"No!" Payton shouted. "I won't!"

"You pathetic child! How dare you defy an elder!" He roared as he advanced on her.

She rose, standing over Terran's lifeless body. She stared directly at Orkat, raised her hands, and pushed the air with force. Like a sonic boom, Orkat was thrown backwards against the wall … and through it! Stone crumbled to the floor and dust filled the air. A roar of pain was followed by silence. Orkat was gone.

Payton knelt down beside Terran. Her tears flooded her eyes.

"Terran?" She whispered "please wake up." A tear fell on his face, and then another. She grabbed his face with both hands, "Terran please …," she begged as one more tear fell.

His eyes popped open. "Terran!" she shrieked, wrapping her arms around his neck.

"Easy, easy!" He said in a weak voice. "I still have to wait a few more minutes before the bruises heal."

"Sorry", she said. She was just so happy that he was okay, she flung her arms around his neck again. "Ah …" he gasped, and then broke into a weak laugh.

Chapter 10

Orkat limped through the door of the council chamber.

Vladok turned away from him in disgust. "You let a female beat you." It was not a question.

"They have started the process of returning her memory to her." Orkat retorted. "That also means her power has begun to return as well. I was not prepared. It won't happen again."

Vladok snorted.

"Let us not forget that fiasco of a raid you led against the Guardians, Vladok!" Lyradis floated forward from one corner of the chamber, "did not go well for either side."

"Damn you Lyradis! You could announce your presence in the room instead of sneaking up like that!" Vladok yelled. He did not like surprises.

"Now, now, dear Vladok. Calm yourself," she cooed. "I'll try to remember." Being the god of darkness and night had great advantages she quite enjoyed. One was sneaking up on the others. Lyradis loved to shock!

"Oh, you're just a little testy about that battle, your loss," she teased. "Oh great god of war and destruction!" Now she was rubbing it in.

"It was not a loss!" he argued.

"What do you call it? A win? A victory? There is no victory when the Guardians still stand!" she shot back.

"Let us not fight amongst ourselves!" a deep commanding voice broke in. Dichune, god of knowledge and power had entered the chamber, behind Orkat. "Calm yourselves and let us focus on the matter at hand." He said.

"Everyone, now, sit down!"

All the Anord sat down at a large round marble table. There were a total of twelve.

Lyradis sat at the same spot she'd always been. She scanned the faces around the table. He stopped at an empty chair directly across from her. Darkness slowly started filling the chamber.

"Lyradis!" Dichune shouted.

She jumped. The darkness faded and light once again filled the room. Lyradis hung her head, a dark fog still surrounding her. "Miss him," she said in an almost inaudible voice.

"Yes, we all do," Dichune soothed, "but we still must discuss our next plan of action. We need your full attention Lyradis. There will come a time when you will have your revenge for your beloved Koris!"

Chapter 11

Terran surveyed the damage to the fortress. “Not too bad. It can be repaired.” He tried to keep his tone a happier one. He did not want to upset her more than she already was. Not after what she’d just been through.

Payton sat on the stairwell watching Terran, her eyes wide, thankful for his full recovery.

He turned to face her, “tell me what happened.” He said. She explained the whole scene from the moment Terran was knocked out. He listened intently.

“So, you now know some of your greatest powers. Sonic boom, healing …”

“Healing?” she broke in. “What do you mean, healing? I didn’t do anything to heal you.”

“Yes, you did,” he said, “your tears, they heal.”

“I thought you could do that on your own! That night … you were beat up bad … I didn’t …,” she was confused.

“Yes, you’re right, I can re-generate on my own. But it takes more time. Your tears heal almost instantly,” he explained, “and as for your sonic boom, I’m glad I was not on the receiving end of it.” Orkat must have been thrown off guard with that one, he thought. There was a slight smile on his lips.

"Is that what it was? I was so angry and scared. He hurt you. I wanted him to just go away," she said, "wanted him to hurt too."

"Oh, I'm sure you hurt him!" Terran replied.

"He felt only a fraction of what you can do. Your power will grow and so will your ability to control it. Orkat knows this. He's probably informed the Anord of this latest development by now."

Terran started pacing the room, thinking, debating whether he should reveal to Payton the next code word. Would it be too soon? Maybe not. It looks like she may need to recall sooner than later. If they were confronted again, and it will happen again, she will need to know what to do.

He stopped, turned and walked to the stairwell. He sat next to Payton, took her hand and asked, "Would you mind if I whispered in your ear again?"

She froze. Her thoughts went back to a few hours ago when Terran last whispered in her ear. The flash, the shaking … the pain.

"Why? I thought you said it was supposed to be a slow process." She said.

"It is, however, Orkat's attack came sooner than anticipated. You will need to be stronger next time. You need to remember how to fight." He said.

Payton thought about what it might feel like. Did she want to feel that pain again so soon? How much more will she recall? Will it be enough? She had so many questions. The code words were the only thing standing in the way. Only Terran knew them, and her parents, and the rest in the Guardian council. How did I know that?

"Are you sure it will help?" she asked.

"Positive." He answered.

"Will you hold me, stay with me until the pain stops?" her eyes welled.

Terran wrapped his arms around her, pulled her close to him. "Of course," he said.

"Okay then," she replied. "Let's get this over with."

Without hesitation, Terran bent down and whispered in her ear, "*Combrac.*"

"Payton's body stiffened, she saw the flash, and the shaking started. She saw the Guardians in council. Her parents were there. They were arguing amongst themselves. Should they send Payton away for her safety, or was she prepared enough to defend herself? Her father was adamant that she be sent away. He feared for her, her mother in tears. As the arguing was still going on, Payton saw a servant refilling goblets of wine. The servant's eyes darted back and forth; he was listening to all that was being said, so intently that he knocked one goblet over spilling the wine all over the table.

There was another flash.

She saw her home. It was a large white limestone castle in the clouds. It positively glowed, with the exception of a large charred mark defacing one wall. It had been a warning from Orkat and his comrades.

Flash.

She was inside the walls. Home. All stop. She slumped into Terran's chest, exhausted. He held her tight.

"Home," she whispered, "take me home, please."

Terran closed his eyes and spoke:

"Here our spirits stand alone
We long for the comfort of home
With swift speed, send us back,
The place we love
To the castle above."

Darkness. Payton could feel their ascension; the darkness was dissipating. She could see light, blue sky, light fluffy clouds. Then it came into view. The home she grew up in. The white limestone walls; the charred mark had been repaired.

She looked up at Terran, "You said a spell; you haven't said any since ….."

"Oh, but I have, my love." He interrupted. "I don't have to say one aloud. I thought we'd enjoy our trip this time. I feel no immediate danger around us."

Terran sent a message to his father through his thoughts. "Father, we're coming home. Contact the Guardians. The Anords have already started to attack. Payton wants to come home."

"We are expecting you, my son," came the reply.

Chapter 12

Payton burst through the large colonial doors. There stood her parents.

"Mother! Father!" She shouted and ran into their waiting arms.

She knew them! As soon as she saw their smiling faces, she remembered. She was so happy. Tears of joy were flooding her eyes and running down her rosy cheeks.

"How I've missed you!" Ardaria cried. Tears were running down her cheeks too.

"My baby!" Liesson choked up, holding Payton so tight she could hardly breathe. She didn't mind.

"Now that's more like it!" A soft voice came from the study doorway. Elrani stood beside Aronon, her arm entwined with his. Terran looked at his parents and strode over to greet both with a huge embrace. "Good to see you and Payton are safe, my son," Aronon said. Elrani's face shone with happiness to see her son alive and well.

All three strode over to Liesson, Ardaria and Payton. Payton embraced Elrani, then Aronon, and with each embrace, there was a flash of recall. She knew them too. She remembered how they accepted and loved her completely as their own daughter when Terran and she were bound. Payton was glad Terran had whispered that code word. She was remembering so much. She was ready to burst.

"As much as I'd like to see this happy homecoming continue," Saer interrupted, "we must meet in the council chambers immediately."

They all filed into the council chambers. Liesson and Ardaria taking their assigned seats as did Elrani and Aronon. Terran and Payton were left, for the moment, to stand in the chamber doorway.

"Please, sit" Saer urged, pointing to the two seats reserved for them. The two sat down in unison. Payton scanned all the faces. So many! There were thirteen gods that made up the Guardians. The faces of her parents, Terran's parents, she knew. The rest looked familiar but she couldn't recall them. Terran could see how confused and frustrated she was.

"Payton, it will come back to you in time. Please try to relax." He said. Her frown faded, she touched his face and gave him a smile, "I will try," she replied.

"Ahem …" Saer cleared his throat. "First, we begin with a welcome back to Terran and Payton. Terran, you have done a wonderful job looking after her and keeping her safe. She has some of her memory back?" he asked. Terran nodded.

"You can ask me Saer!" Payton shot back at him. "I can speak, you know!"

"And I see you still have your strong will!" he chuckled. "I apologize Payton, I will direct my questions about you, to you."

"Thank you." She answered, a little indignantly. Suddenly recalling she had called him by his name. She smiled to herself. Terran tapped her knee; he caught it too. Saer continued, raising his left eyebrow at Payton. "We have recently discovered a spy in our midst." Shocked gasps and eyes were large. "Who?" someone asked. Payton did not see who it was.

"Our servant, Rokan. I found that his interests in our meetings became more intense. In our last one, he disappeared from the chamber rather quickly after we discussed the possibility of bringing Payton back to us. I followed him to his quarters and caught him with note in hand. A note to the Anords. It said, and I quote,

"She will be home soon. Will contact when she arrives.

Rokan"

"Traitor!" Liesson roared, slamming his fist on the large marble table so hard, Payton thought it would break!

"Calm yourself Liesson!" Ardaria said. "He was caught!"

"What have you done with him?" Liesson demanded.

"We have locked him up in the lowest level of Lugan Prison. If we put him any lower, he will speak to Hades himself." Saer answered. "And," he continued, "he confessed to his treachery. He will be in Lugan for a very long time."

"Why don't you release him to me? I'll take him for a little hunt in the forest," Hiar piped up, "should be entertaining."

Hiar was the god of the hunt and forests. He loved a good hunt. Although he preferred to hunt deer or elk, he would make an exception for this human.

"How much did he know?" Niamut, god of knowledge and wisdom, asked.

"Plenty!" Saer answered. "In fact, he knew that we had thirteen code words that would bring back Payton's memory. Twelve of these, words we all know. The thirteenth is known only to Terran." All eyes fell on Terran. He shifted in his seat a little. It was un-nerving to have thirteen of the most powerful gods stare at you.

"To continue," Saer broke in, "he also knew that after Terran reveals the final code word to Payton, she would be vulnerable for at least three minutes. That is plenty of time for the Anords to steal her power. She will have full knowledge of her power and her memory; however, it will take those few minutes for all to take effect."

"I have revealed three to her already," Terran said, "and I'm sure I will have to reveal more sooner than planned." There were random nods of agreement. Payton was uneasy. All this fuss and she couldn't help, not yet anyway. Niamut stood from the marble table and slowly walked over to Payton. He was directly behind her when he announced, "We must prepare for battle. It will be upon us soon. Terran, you will have to prepare Payton. Remind her how to fight." Niamut put his hand on her shoulder, "My dear," he said, "pay attention to what Terran teaches you in the next few days. Learn fast, learn well, for we will need you and your skills in the battle to come. Liesson!" Niamut's attention now directed to her father, as was hers. "You have the Great Treaty?" he asked.

"It is safe" Liesson answered. He would not elaborate as to where it was.

"Very well," Saer broke in, "we will adjourn for now. Keep alert!"

Chapter 13

Terran led Payton through the chamber door. Payton glanced back to see all were on their feet, her parents smiling, but they did not move.

Terran closed the door behind them. “Come, we’ll have a bite to eat and then rest.” He said.

“Why aren’t the rest coming out too; I thought this meeting was over.” She asked.

“For us, it is.” He replied.

Chapter 14

After what seemed like a veritable feast for many, consisting of three different meats, a variety of salads, pastas and vegetables, Terran and Payton retired to a huge master bedroom.

Payton flopped down on the bed and let out a sign. “Uh, I’m so full! I ate way too much, but it was so good! I didn’t realize I was so hungry!”

“Yeah, no kidding” Terran teased.

“Hey!” she balked. Terran was still snickering.

He walked over to the bed and flopped down beside her. She was giggling. He turned, and propped himself up on one arm, facing her. He loved watching her laugh. He wanted her to be happy. Just for her to be happy, whatever it took.

Payton turned toward him, still giggling, and reached out and touched his face. The giggling stopped. He bent down and kissed her gently. She felt herself melting.

“Stop!”

“Correct me, but aren’t you supposed to start teaching me how to fight?” Payton asked.

Terran let out a rather large sigh, “Yes.”

“So, let’s start!” She was eager to regain the skills she had forgotten when her memory was ‘messed with’.

"You need to get a couple of hours of sleep Payton. We've been doing a lot of 'jumping;' – your word, and you've had three awakenings. I know you're tired. Hell, I'm tired." said Terran.

"Ha! Your mind was not on sleep a few seconds ago!" No sooner had she said the words, fatigue started to set in on her. She was exhausted. "Wow, I am … so … tired," she whispered, yawning. She laid her head on a soft pillow and drifted off to sleep.

Chapter 15

Dream

Light, bright, almost iridescent,light.

Floating, I'm floating. Payton looked down at the large puffy clouds beneath her feet. Blue sky and white clouds. How beautiful. Her awe was interrupted with a CRASH followed by a bright flash and thunder. She spun around. Fighting! There was a battle going on right in front of her. She saw her father, Liesson. His battle armour, shining white, was fighting with another man. 'Another god!' She was frozen in place. All she could do was watch. Her father, large and strong, lunged toward his enemy, Koris. She knew, somehow. In an instant, Koris seemed to disappear in a small, but fierce, snow storm. Wind whipped the snow in a total white-out. Liesson, a warrior of combat, anticipated Koris' move, and whipped around the small blizzard. Koris was famous for his blizzards. He confused and disorientated his enemies with them. When they were in this state, Koris would blast them with a stream of ice, encasing the victim in solid ice. But Liesson knew. He managed to stay at the edge of the blizzard. He saw a glimpse of Koris' back. He was slowly turning, searching for his victim, Liesson. Just as they made eye contact, Koris felt it. Cold steel. He fell to his knees. The storm faded quickly, and he was now face-to-face with

Liesson. Payton heard the two men's voices, in whispers, but she could hear every word.

"We will win Liesson," Koris gasped for air.

"Not while the Guardians live," Liesson replied. "It doesn't have to be this way. We can, once again, be in harmony."

"No!" Koris gasped again. "Tired of being shadows ... you are God of Honor ... give me a true death. Not this ... slow ..." Koris raised his head, looked straight into Liesson's eyes. The flash of the blade was the last thing Koris saw before his head was separated from his body.

"No! ......" Payton turned to see Lyradis running for Koris. She fell on her knees beside his body, sobbing. "You will pay, Liesson!" she was screaming at him now. Tears were streaming down her face. "You will pay!"

Liesson walked away slowly. Not uttering a word. The battle had stopped the instant Koris was beheaded. All of them stood in complete shock. No God was ever killed before. All Anords vanished, taking Koris' body with them.

Ardaria was standing beside Liesson, a sad look on her face.

"No one has ever slain a god" she said. "Gods have never battled like this before," Liesson said quietly.

All Guardians were now together in a circle.

"Only a god can kill another god," Saer said firmly, his lips pressed into a thin line.

"Let us not forget this."

Payton awoke with a start. She stood straight up in bed. Her eyes wide. She was searching, searching … for what? She thought.

The dream. That's what it was, a dream. She rubbed her eyes and shook her head a bit. Wake up Payton, she thought.

Breathe, she told herself. Let out a long slow breathe, and forced herself to relax. Her eyes closed; quiet. Nice calming quiet.

Chapter 16

Dichune sat at the head of the long marble table, slowly looking at each empty chair. There were six on either side. "All great gods," he thought. One missing – Koris. How could such a mighty god fall?

We Anords must find a way to defeat the Guardians, he thought. We must keep them apart. At least until I figure out how I can bring both to the Anords. Once we have total power, the Gods of all the Earth will have no choice but to fall on their knees to us. And we, at last, will be all powerful.

"Even you, Zeus. You will kneel to me." Dichune whispered.

He hated Zeus, and his brothers. They were powerful. Not more powerful than any other, but powerful none the less.

Dichune hated their arrogance, hated them all.

A loud knock at the chamber door shook Dichune from his thoughts.

"Enter" he said.

The large wooden doors opened, and Vladok walked through, close behind him was Lis.

Lis quickly walked ahead of Vladok and stopped short, making Vladok bump her slightly. He snarled. "Oh wipe that look off your face!" she sang. "You're much more handsome when you smile Vladok. "Hmph" he retorted. "Lis, have you forgotten that I know when you're lying?"

In fact, Vladok knew he was not a handsome god at all. But, he didn't mind. In fact, he quite enjoyed it. To appear as a ghostly image to a human gave him such satisfaction. The fear in that puny human's face just made his day.

Lis giggled. She just couldn't resist. What's the point of being the god of lies and treason if you couldn't enjoy your powers!

"What do you want?" Dichune yelled. "I'm busy!"

"Oh, but I see you are!" Lis quipped. "Not!"

"Lis, don't. I'm not in the mood," Dichune said.

"Oh, okay," Lis said, "but I believe we have something that will brighten your day."

"Let go you jerk!" Orkat strolled in, sword in one hand, a woman in the other. She was struggling violently, trying to break free, cursing wildly.

"And what is that?" Dichune asked, still annoyed.

"Dichune, have a closer look," Orkat said.

"Fine."

Dichune stood up and walked over to Orkat, who still had the young woman hanging in the air. He got closer, slowly walked around the two of them, then stopped right in front of her.

"You can put her down Orkat. There's nowhere for her to run." He said. Orkat let the woman down. She stood glaring at Dichune.

"What the hell is this? Who are you people?" she was furious. Dichune could almost see the fire in her eyes. He stepped back.

No. It couldn't be! "Where did you find her?" Dichune asked eyes wide with delight.

"Checked out some of the covens, and found that old hag Helgen was hiding her. Wanted to keep her as a pet, Helgen said. Stupid old hag." Vladok said.

"Wonderful! Well done! Dichune said. He hadn't been this happy in a long time. Finally, some leverage. He turned back to the woman and smiled.

"Lilith."

Chapter 17

"There it is." whispered Aronon, "Helgen's lair."

Rekor nodded. Both stood before an old house that looked like it was ready to fall over. Aronon knew it was a spell to make the place look run down and abandoned. "Helgen is good at her spells." he said, "Anyone coming by here wouldn't want to stay and look around. Looks like hell!"

"Let's just get this over with." Rekor said. Rekor didn't care for Helgen. A wretched old hag. Most miserable witch he'd ever met. Looked a hundred plus in years, white stringy hair, it almost shone in the dark, hunched over, wrinkled face, long crooked nose. Your typical witch you heard about in fairy tales.

She actually tried to put a spell on Rekor once. He laughed quietly. Spells don't work on gods. Witches and warlocks may have their power, but they are still human.

"Looks a little too quiet," Aronon broke Rekor's train of thought, "ah hell, we'd better check it out."

Both rushed to the front door and burst in. Nothing. Still too quiet.

"What do you want now?" Helgen yelled through the darkness. "You've already taken just about everything I have."

Aronon lit up the room with a simple spell and saw her sitting in a corner hugging her spell book. Aronon knew it was her most prized possession.

"Well, you've managed to hold onto your spells," he said.

"Yes, I have … barely." She said. "Everything else is gone! Have you any idea how long it will take me to gather ingredients, candles, pots! So much lost. Eye of newt is not easy to acquire. They're so small and they put up one hell of a fight, and …"

"Helgen!' Rekor interrupted.

Helgen stared at him, wishing she could curse him with the evil eye.

"We don't care what you've lost Helgen. We have information that you've been hiding a young woman. Where is she?" Rekor demanded.

"Haven't you overbearing gods done enough? She's gone! Your friends came for her." Helgen cackled. She stood up and shuffled closer to Aronon.

"You're too late Aronon." She said, her smile growing wider. "She's in their hands now. Things are going to get tough. How are you going to get her back now?" Helgen was laughing.

Rekor started for her, he wanted her to feel the hardness of power.

"Rekor," Aronon stepped in front of him "please stop," he said. "She can't help us. The damage is already done. We have to tell the others. They will not be happy." Both men turned and left the house; left Helgen muttering to herself. Cursing the day she ever got involved with the gods.

Chapter 18

Flash! Rekor and Aronon were back in the Guardians fortress. This flash flight was never Aronon's thing. Yes, it was fast, convenient, but curses if it didn't turn a mortal's stomach. He had no choice. He knew Rekor would not let him use his own methods as he found them to be too slow. Although Aronon quite liked his broom!

"Did you find her?" Liesson asked. "Anords got to her first," replied Rekor. "Damn, damn, damn!" roared Liesson, smashing his fist on the corner of the marble table.

"Calm yourself Liesson," Ardaria said. "We will find a way."

Liesson let out a large sigh. They had to bring her back to Lugan Prison. It's the only place that could hold her. Lilith had no idea who she was. He was hoping it would stay that way. For now. If she found out, existence for all gods and mortals would become very difficult.

Payton strolled along the hall, enjoying the scenery. So many magnificent paintings – of gods, no doubt – and large, beautiful statues. Some she'd recognized as her father, Liesson, her mother Ardaria, Elrani, Rekor, Niamut, Hiar, Saer and … Orkat? What's this, she thought. She saw Vladok, Lyradis and Dichune, and a few more she didn't know. She was trying her best to re-familiarize herself with the ones she was supposed to know. Or so she thought. Some of these gods tried to kill her! Or at least one! Orkat. Why? She wished she knew more. That she could remember more. The erasing of her memory was frustrating. At times, exhausting! She felt something inside missing. Something more than just her memory … but what? She walked over to a large door, open just a crack. She heard voices, talking, sometimes yelling. She stopped just outside the door. Listening. Now it was quiet inside. Then she heard Saer.

"We will convene tonight. Call all Guardians. We must come up with a plan to bring Lilith to us."

"I will put the call out immediately, Saer," said Elrani.

"Where's Payton now?" Ardaria asked. "Resting," Aronon said. "Terran's with her."

"Good. I don't want her to know about Lilith yet. She is not prepared." said Ardaria.

They all agreed then dispersed to prepare for the meeting that evening.

Payton backed away from the door, backed right into the wall behind her. They're keeping even more secrets from me, she thought. Lilith, who's this Lilith, and what does she have to do with me?

She started back toward her room, questions rolling around in her head. Terran, maybe he can answer them. No, he can't. Or won't, is more like it. Need to know, need to know! Maybe Terran will whisper another word in her ear. Maybe then she'll know more. Those words, they were a different language, yet she knew what they meant. And the pain that followed. It didn't last long, but it was the most intense pain she'd ever felt. The one thing she didn't look forward to.

Chapter 19

"Just get in there!" Orkat ordered as he pushed the confused, yet very angry young woman in the cell.

Lilith's eyes darted around a dark and damp cave-like room.

"Some cell. It's a bloody hole in the ground!" she screamed. "Why do people keep hiding me in holes?"

"I think it would be better if you calmed down a little, Lilith," Dichune said. "Then maybe we may explain things to you in a civil manor."

Even the sound of Dichune's voice grated on Lilith's nerves. Who the hell does he think he is? Overbearing, condescending, jerk, she thought. Her anger was all she knew. It's what kept her going and alive on the streets in London. The lying, cheating, and stealing felt good. It gave her a rush. She even killed a few, usually when they put up a fight when she robbed them. She was never caught. She was very good at her chosen profession, even proud of herself at being a master at it. Although, she didn't quite figure out how she got to the streets. She just seemed to appear there one stormy night. She didn't give it much thought until she ran into, what she thought was another homeless old woman wandering the dark streets. This will be an easy target, she thought. No one would care if a homeless old woman was found dead in the alley. Whatever meagre possessions she had, missing. She was wrong. When Lilith confronted the old woman, the hag looked up at her, smiled and grabbed Lilith's left wrist tight, wrapped a gold, thorny vine around it. The thorns dug into her wrist. The pain was excruciating, and she dropped to one knee. The old woman then wrapped the vine around her right wrist. It made Lilith cry out in pain, and she fell down to the ground.

"Hello my dear," the old hag said softly, "I think I should take you home." Lilith heard the old hag cackle, grab the vine between her wrists and drag her down the street. The pain made Lilith pass out.

She awoke in a small dark room in an old, rundown house. Hands still bound with the gold vine. She would demand that the binds be removed to no avail. The old hag would cackle and say, "It's not safe to do that!"

Now I end up here in a dark room again, watching this Dichune guy pace back and forth.

'*He wants me to calm down? Fine! I'll calm down. He better start talking soon. I'm losing my patience fast,*' she thought.

She let out a large sigh and sat down on the large wooden chair against the left wall, the only chair in the room.

"Well?" she asked. Eyes fixed on Dichune. Fire still shone in them. Dichune stopped his pacing and turned to face her.

"Lilith, you've been brought to us for a very special task," he began. "We've had some difficulty finding you, but …"

"So get on with it already" she snapped.

“Keep your tongue, young lady or I’ll have Orkat here wrap the golden vine around your throat!” said Dichune. Lilith opened her mouth to fight back, but closed it again, recalling the pain the vine caused.

“May I continue?” Dichune asked. “Good. Now, you Lilith are part of a very special being. You are, shall I say, the evil half of a very special being. You do not remember how you came to be, although, you do wonder.”

Lilith nodded.

“You came to be, as a result of a battle between the Guardians and ourselves, the Anords. During the battle, one being – which you are a part of – could not bear the thought of our world falling apart. This is our theory. Her pain inside her so great, she somehow, literally, became two. No sooner had it happened, you disappeared.”

“Okay, so who and what am I?” Lilith asked, through clenched teeth.

“You, my dear, are a god.” Dichune answered. “Or part of one, that is.”

Lilith’s eyes widened, mouth dropped for a moment, then she regained herself, “Uh huh. Right.” She retorted. Now she was laughing to herself.

“You laugh, but it is the truth.” said Dichune.

Chapter 20

Payton opened the door to her bed chamber. Terran was still asleep. Good. He looked so peaceful when he slept, and so handsome of course. She wanted to climb back into bed and snuggle up to him. No, I can't. I need to find out who Lilith is, and why people are keeping secrets from me, she thought. She wished she could remember …. Remember. "Ahah!" Payton said. Ooops – that was louder than she had intended it to be. She turned to see if Terran had awoken to her shout. He was still asleep.

"Whew."

The archives room. She remembered Terran pointing it out when he was showing her the palace. But could she find it again?

Entering the adjoining bathroom, Payton reached for the brush on the counter. She quickly brushed through her hair, checked her face and walked back to the chamber, heading straight for the dresser. She opened the top drawer, and then paused – wait a minute. She didn't have to do this the usual way. She still had the habits of her old human life lingering inside her. She closed the dresser drawer and stepped back from it. Okay, I'll try this on a conscious level. Last time she hadn't even realized what she had done. She closed her eyes and thought, jeans, blue, … no white t-shirt, and tan ankle boots.

She felt it. She had clothes on. She ran back into the bathroom to check. Yep. Clothes she thought of were on her, but something didn't feel right. Oh, that's it! Payton saw herself blushing in the mirror. One quick thought and voila! Underwear. She laughed at herself. She didn't know gods could blush.

Scanning herself in the mirror again; presentable!

Walking out of the bathroom, heading to the door, she glanced back one more time at the bed. Terran was still sleeping.

Payton peeked around the open door. There was no one in sight. She stepped into the hallway, closed the door behind her and continued down the hallway, walking as quietly as she could, checking each room to see if it was the archives room she'd been searching for. Archives, archives … where is it? Just as the frustration was starting to set in, there it was! The door to the archives room. 'Cartlann' was the word carved into the wood of the door. She somehow knew what it meant. Glancing up and down the hall one more time – no one. Good! She grabbed he door knob and turned it. Inside the room, Payton scanned the walls. There were thousands of books, scrolls, and papers. Where to start! Well, let's hope that things are in alphabetical order, she thought.

They weren't. From what she could figure out, the order was according to date.

Wars, disease, feuds, judgements, history as far back as she could imagine. Everything was written down, in every language too. Latin, Egyptian, Greek, Chinese, Arabic and more.

She searched for something she might find more familiar to her.

And there it was. A book, a rather large book on its own pedestal. It had white, gold and black trim. On the cover, in bold letters, and in beautiful script, was one word – '*Coimirceoir.*'

Guardians – she just knew. This is it!

Payton carefully opened the book and started to read.

Chapter 21

The entries were made by Erean. Who's Erean? Never mind. Ok.

There is dissention amongst the Gods. The Anords grow increasingly tired of their role in our world. Toros does nothing to ease the tension. He sits back and smiles, with pride. His flock is strong, he thinks, but not stronger than mine. We must have equality in our world and the world of the humans. If we fail, the mortal world will fall into great upheaval. The Anords desire a world of war and misery and more. The Guardians must try to prevent such a world. There is only one hope …

"Payton!"

She jumped and screamed, turning from the book to see Terran standing in the doorway.

"What are you doing in here? How did you get in this room? The door is always locked!" Terran said, looking a little frantic. In seconds, he was facing her. Payton, still in shock, didn't move. She just stared at him. Terran reached around her and closed the large book.

"I … I …" she stammered, unable to finish.

"I'm sorry I frightened you Payton," Terran apologized. "I was very shocked to find you in this room."

She relaxed.

"I heard the others talking. They … they didn't know I was listening." She explained, "They are keeping secrets. I want … no – need, to know more! I heard them mention," she hesitated, "Lilith."

Terran's eyes widened for a split second. Then, he tried, in vain, to change the look on his face. It was too late. Payton caught it.

"Who's Lilith?" she asked.

"I can't tell you right now," he answered. "If I did, it would alter the path we need to take for you to regain your memory and your role in our world. We must follow the rules precisely."

"So get on with it then!" She demanded. "Whisper another one of those words in my ear and let me get on with things!"

"I told you, I can't do that yet. I've already said three of them, sooner than I was supposed to." He said.

"Argh" she threw her hands up in frustration and headed for the door, down the hallway, heading back to the bedroom. She knew she should be furious, but she wasn't. Frustrated, that's it. Just plain frustrated. She paced. Within a few minutes, Terran was back in the bedroom also.

"And who's Erean?" she asked, still pacing. "He is the leader of all Guardians" he answered. "I thought that was my father," she was confused.

"Your father is his right hand, so to speak. He reports – and only he – to Erean."

"And Toros?"

"The leader of the Anords," Terran answered.

"Okay, fine." She said. She started for the bedroom door but Terran stepped in front of her.

"Where are you going now?" he asked.

"To the training room," she said. "If you can't tell me more, I'll have to grab a few things, and find out for myself." She pushed past him, headed out the door and headed straight for the training room, Terran, behind her, trying to convince her otherwise. But, she wasn't listening.

Let's see now – gazing at all the weaponry that was available. She didn't want anything too big or heavy. She wanted to travel light. She grabbed a small curved dagger. Could do some damage if she needed to use it. There, two arm bands – metal and large enough to protect her forearms – snapping one on each arm. Perfect fit! She spotted a sword. Not too large – good! She grabbed it and wrapped the belt, the weapon was attached to, around her waist. Rope, she wanted rope. Not sure why – just thought it was needed. Ah! She spotted a shiny gold rope with thorns on it. Unusual rope, but it'll have to do. She attached it the belt. There! Admiring herself in the mirror on the wall, she wished she felt as formidable as she looked.

"Payton, please don't do this," Terran begged. "It's too dangerous."

"Then come with me. Aren't you supposed to protect me?" she said. "Look, I'm going stir-crazy. There are things I'm allowed to know, and things I'm not allowed to know … yet. I need to train, but I'm not sure what I'm training for! Sure, I need to know how to protect myself, but …""I'm coming with you," Terran replied. "Let me grab a few things."

"Thought warlocks didn't need weapons – got your spells and tricks." She smiled.

"Never know" he smiled back.

Chapter 22

"Ahhh!"

Lilith hit the floor with a loud thud.

"Come now, girl!" Orkat barked. "You must have more than that!" He was smiling now. With all the fire and anger in this girl, he expected more. More strength, more cunning, something! It was amusing him though. Again, he was smiling.

"Wipe that smile off your face!" Lilith screamed.

"Give me a reason little girl," he said. He was starting to laugh … Lilith flipped back on her feet, with quick darting movements, she grabbed a dagger, whipped around Orkat and stopped just short of Orkat's eye. A shiny tip of steel was so close that if he blinked, the sharp tip would slice his eyelid.

"Bravo, my dear." Lilith turned to see Vladok walking towards her, clapping his hands. Orkat backed away from the dagger tip still aimed at his eye.

"It appears that the real skill reveals itself when you are very angry. We must now concentrate that anger." He said. Lilith, with the dagger still in her hand, let her arm fall to her side. She was staring at Vladok.

"Okay, wipe that stupid look off your face, girl!" he snapped. "I see I need to clarify. The only good results from you, in the art of combat, is when you are extremely angry. Use that anger. In every movement, every thought, every decision, in everything. Only then will you be able to fight effectively."

"I hear you," she said, "jerk" quietly.

"Heard you," said Vladok. He turned, headed for the wall of weaponry displayed. He chose a spear. Double headed; one end had your typical shiny pointed end and the other end had a long, curved blade. He took the spear down, grabbed it with both hands, turned to face Lilith and said, "Defend yourself!"

Vladok lunged at her. She moved just in time to see the spear tip smash into the floor. She ran for the weapons, her anger starting to build again. "That bastard!" Lilith leapt straight into the wall, grabbed a sword, and flipped, somersaulting in the air, landing on both feet, facing Vladok.

"Come on!" she screamed.

Vladok lunged again, this time with the blade end. Lilith leapt straight up just as he swung it at her. It missed her, barely. Landing on her feet again, now she was dodging, darting, back and forth, evading the weapon in Vladok's hands. Just as she was about to be cornered, she ducked; another swing of the blade. She darted, quickly, between Vladok's legs. She jumped up on his shoulders, blade to his throat.

"Ha! Got ya!" She said.

"Very good, my dear," Vladok replied. He could feel her grip relax slightly. He grabbed her arm and flipped her down on the floor with a loud thud.

"You let your guard down. Never let your guard down. The ones you fight will know how to fight. They will try to find weakness. You must not let them find any. Ever!"

"Now," he said turning his attention to Orkat, "teach her properly. Stop this cat and mouse game. She needs to be prepared!"

"She should know combat already," Orkat retorted. "This is a waste of time."

"Orkat, she has no memory of it and we have to re-train her. Her skills are there; teach her how to use them." Vladok said. He dropped the spear, turned and walked out of the training room.

Orkat turned to face Lilith. "Ok girl, let's see what you got." He lunged.

Chapter 23

Flash!

Payton and Terran were back in Egypt. “See, I told you, you could do it!” Terran said, smiling widely. He was impressed at how fast Payton was regaining her skills – at least some of them. He’d hoped, though, that it would be more gradual. She seemed to be doing more, even without the code words. This worried him. He could see the expression her face – the intense jabs of pain. Just for a split second.

“Yea, thanks” she said. “I feel a little weak.”

“You will until you regain all memory.” He told her.” You have power, but not all of it. That will come in time, and we can’t rush this. I let you try flash flight on your own, and it worked, however, I saw that look on your face. Hurt, didn’t it?”

Payton nodded.

“So, we’ll rest for a few moments; figure out our next move,” he said. Payton sat down on the hard granite bench. ‘We’re in Cleo’s crypt again,’ she thought, wondering why they came back. She rested her head in her hands. Still a little dizzy. ‘Rest’ he says. She wasn’t going to rest long. Whether he liked it or not, she was going to find some answers.

They left the ‘fortress,’ as Terran called it. She preferred ‘palace.’ That sounded more pleasant.

They left the palace in a hurry. Payton didn't want the other gods to know what she had in mind. If they knew, she was sure they would try to stop her. She didn't like defying her parents. She didn't like that her parents were keeping important information from her. It must be important. Why were they all holding back? Surely the more she knew, the more she could help.

"So," she started, "I know one thing. I need to find Lilith, whoever she is, and talk to her."

"There's no rush," said Terran.

"No rush ...," she said, staring straight into Terran's eyes. He quickly looked away.

"There's something about this woman; which obviously has to do with me. Wish I knew what, but something in me tells me that I need to find her." She said, still staring at him. He started to feel uneasy. Terran calmed himself. 'Change your demeanour or she won't stop,' he thought.

"Payton, relax will you?" he said. "Your parents, my parents, all the others, are working on it."

"Working on what? From what I can figure out, I'm supposedly this 'chosen one,' there was a battle, I get sent away, memory erased; you find me and bring me back, tell me you can bring back my memory – very slowly, I might add, and ..."

"Alright already," Terran interrupted. "I get your point. I know the story."

"Lilith," Payton said. "Tell me."

Chapter 24

Thirteen Guardians gathered in the meeting room, mulling around, murmuring to each other. Events were moving faster than any of them had anticipated.

Liesson went to the head of the table. “Everyone?” he spoke loudly, “please take your seats.”

The rest moved to their chairs and sat down. All eyes were fixed on Liesson.

“Liesson, what has Erean said? Do we move forward sooner than we expected?” asked Amachtera, god of sun and day.

Liesson sighed, “Yes Amachtera, we do. In fact, we must.” The silence was deafening.

“Erean has tried,” he continued, “to reason with Toros. It was in vain. Toros is determined. He is filled with so much confidence. Toros says that our reign in this world will soon be over. He has told Erean to prepare for the end. We cannot let this happen.” Liesson looked at Ardaria, his eyes sad and dark.

“We must prepare ourselves for possible sacrifice.”

Ardaria’s expression changed to shock. “No, Liesson, we can’t!”

Liesson bowed his head and said, “The Anords will be ready to strike soon, my love. If we don’t stop them, they will see to it Payton never becomes the god we all hoped for. That is her birthright." Liesson looked up; looked at all the gods gazing back.

"We will have to have Terran speak the next code word to Payton and hope she is strong enough to receive it." Liesson looked at Elrani, and moved his gaze back to Ardaria.

He was worried. He didn't want to sacrifice his only daughter, his only child. He couldn't bear it, he knew. It would destroy Ardaria. They had no choice. The fate of their world and the mortals of their world were at stake.

"Find Terran," he ordered, "and Payton. Bring them here. Erean has ordered me to tell Payton her fate. We have no choice." He ended in a whisper.

"My lords!" Myshana, servant to the Guardians, burst through the door. "My lords – forgive my interruption."

"What is it Myshana?" Liesson asked. "A note," she replied, waving the paper in the air, "from Terran. I found it on the door of the Cartlann room!"

Myshana ran over and handed the note to Liesson. He read it quickly. "Oh no!"

"What is it Liesson?" Ardaria asked.

"Payton," he said "she found the archives room, and the 'Leabhar'." He read the note aloud.

Payton found the Ór Leabhar Caradiunn. I stopped before she could read too far. I've taken her away from here, where I can keep her safe. Will contact you as soon as I am able.

I'm sorry. I've failed you. I should have kept a closer eye on her.

Forgive me,

Terran

Silence swept the room once again. Myshana broke the silence. "My lords?"

"Thank you Myshana," Liesson said to her. "You may go." Myshana left the room.

"Aronon" said Liesson. "Use your magic. Call for Terran. We must find them before the Anords find them. The rest of you, prepare for battle. "Like it or not," Erean said, "tomorrow … we fight, once again."

Chapter 25

'Divine Goddess, Goddess divine,

Divine God, God divine,

If evil appears within these walls,

I beg you,

Banish evil for the protection of all'

Terran walked around the crypt chanting the same spell three times. When he was finished, he sat beside Payton on the stone bench, slipped his arm around her waist, and pulled her close.

"There," he said, "that should do for a while."

"Thought magic didn't work on Gods," said Payton.

"Ah yes, but I am half god," Terran replied. "My spells work to a certain extent." Payton looked at him, not saying a word, expecting more of an explanation … "Okay, okay," he said. "What I mean is, it takes longer for a full God to break through my spells, because I am half god. Oh, they can break through, but it is difficult. It's the one power my father doesn't have." Terran smiled. It took him years to develop his skills as a wizard. His father, Aronon, was stern. Made Terran practice for hours, almost to total exhaustion, every day.

The day Terran's full power revealed itself was when he tried a small spell on his mother Elrani. She had walked into the training room, intending to observe her son as he practiced his magic. He was nowhere to be found. She saw Aronon standing alone in the middle of the room but no Terran. Searching the room, she suddenly felt a tap on her shoulder. She spun around. Nothing. It happened again and again. No one was there. She smiled and called "Terran …" No answer. She was waving her hand in a small circle in the air, a slight flick of her fingers. Nothing. The motion should have broken any spell instantly. She tried several times, when finally Terran fell from the ceiling, just a few feet in front of her, laughing. Aronon then broke his silence, laughing so hard, he fell to his knees. Finally, Aronon and Terran got up off the floor. Aronon put his arms around Terran's shoulders. "He's done it, my dear." He said. "He's surpassed me. I'm so proud!" Elrani smiled brightly. She too, was so proud of her son. "How wonderful!" She exclaimed.

Terran knew he and Payton couldn't stay in Cleo's crypt for long. The Anords and Guardians would be searching for them. But, where to go. Think man, think! He thought of asking the Egyptian god Horace for help, but knew it would be risky. Where Horace was, Anubis wasn't far behind and the gods of other lands didn't want to get involved with gods outside their realm. They didn't want to believe that this war brewing between the Guardians and Anords had any impact on them. This was just the beginning, Terran knew. If the Guardians fell, it was a matter of time before the gods of all the lands on Earth – the good gods – would fall also. The Anords would destroy all the good in the world.

"Terran," Payton said his name, breaking his train of thought. He loved it when she said his name, loved the sound of her voice. He loved her more than anything.

"I lost you for a moment," she said. "Sorry love," he said, bringing her closer to him and kissing her softly.

"You're trying to distract me," she said softly.

"Uh huh," he said, going in for another kiss. He stopped just before their lips met. Froze.

"Terran?" Payton said.

He was frozen. He could faintly hear Payton's voice calling his name, but he couldn't answer. His father's voice and image flooded his mind.

'Terran, son, where are you?' Aronon asked.

'Safe, father.' Terran answered, 'for now.'

'Terran, you must bring Payton back to the fortress. Erean has commanded we take measures to give Payton her memories now.' Aronon told him. 'Things are worse than expected. Terran, we go to battle tomorrow.'

'Father, no!' Terran pleaded. 'It may kill her!'

'I'm so sorry son, we have no choice … Erean commands it. It's a chance we have to take,' said Aronon. 'We'll see you and Payton soon. Please Terran – bring her back.'

Terran moved, his father's voice and image vanishing from his mind.

"Terran!" Payton's panicked voice was now loud and clear. "Terran, what happened? Are you okay?"

"Yeah … yeah, I'm good." He answered. "Payton, we have to go back home," he said.

"Why?" She questioned, "we just got here. You're supposed to help me get some answers."

"I know, maybe this will help." He said.

Terran leaned in close, whispering in her ear, "I'm sorry – I have to do this love, …. Urraim."

Pain … so much pain. Payton slid off the stone bench to her knees on the floor. Stars, she actually saw stars, dancing, sparkling , a dark night sky, so dark, yet she could see clearly. There was a figure in the stars, larger than life calling her name. Who was this? Erean! Is it Erean? More pain. She collapsed to the floor holding her head in her hands. I hear you Erean, I hear you. Darkness.

"Payton … Payton!" Terran was almost frantic. "Wake up – come on, Payton, please … wake up …"

Payton stirred, moving very slowly, both hands went to either side of her head; moaning, mumbling "Erean …"

"She'd never had such a pounding headache, more like the mother of all migraines! She felt beat up, could hardly move. Get up, she thought. Terran's freaking out and you don't have the strength to answer. Payton gave him a faint smile, trying to reassure him. He calmed down a little.

"Oh, okay," Terran said while lifting her up and sitting her back down on the stone bench. "We're going, as soon as you get your strength back." Now he was pacing back and forth.

"No" she said weakly.

"Yes."

"No!" she snapped.

Payton sighed, "We can't go back. I won't! Not yet!"

Flash! She was gone.

"Payton, NO!" Terran called out, reaching out to where she stood. "NO!!!"

Chapter 26

Bright light! Flash!

Payton was standing. *I'm still standing.* Wow! She recovered from the last memory word quicker than usual. She thought. Alone. She was totally alone. Since the night she helped Terran recover from the attack on him, she'd never been alone. Now, she was on her own. But where to start?

'Father!' Terran threw his thoughts out to Aronon harder and faster than he'd ever done.

'I'm here,' Aronon replied.

'Father, she's gone! She left me standing here. She flashed on her own! What do I do?' Terran was frantic again.

'Slow down, son. She left on her own? She's not ready for what or who she might run into.'

'I know. Help, please!' Terran pleaded.

'Yes, yes, give me a minute.' His father said. 'The after-burn – can you detect it?'

'Yes.'

'Good,' said Aronon, 'good. Now, concentrate – where did she go?'

Terran stood in the exact spot Payton had been before she flashed. A faint scent, he could detect it now. So soft and flowery – a scent that only she had. Every God had their own scent in the after-burn left behind. Payton's was one that Terran would never forget. It lingered. He sighed.

'Terran,' he heard his father's voice again.

'East' Terran told him, 'somewhere east, but I can't pinpoint it. Argh, this is so frustrating!'

'Good thing you are a half-breed my boy,' said Aronon. 'You must try to find her before the Anords find her. Start now. We have no time to waste. And Terran, … don't forget to keep me posted, often.'

Terran agreed.

Flash – he left the crypt.

Payton scanned the country-side. It was beautiful. Mountains, flowers, trees as far as the eye could see. She was in awe of it all. How could anyone, mortal or god, want to destroy such beauty?

The mountains, they looked familiar. Carpathians! She was in Romania! How could she have come here? Her thoughts before she flashed were of Lilith – she had to find Lilith. That must be it. 'Whatever or whoever I think of before I flash, that's where I'll end up! Her thoughts were going faster. What if she's close? Has she seen me?' Payton ducked behind a large bush. Peaked out to see anyone was watching. She scanned the area more closely. There was no one around. Whew. Good! 'Now, something tells me I'm in the right place. Well, obviously not exactly the right place, but I'm close. I can feel it!'

She turned and started toward the mountains, somehow knowing this was the path to take. As she hiked along, her thoughts were racing. If there were witches, warlocks, and gods in this world, do other beings exist also? The fairy tales, were they just stories, or were they true events converted to fairy tales, to divert the mortal world? Ogres, werewolves, fairies, vampires … was it all true? She kept her guard up as she walked along. Scanning every tree, every bush, the long grass mixed with beautiful wild flowers. She kept a slow steady pace. Still weak from the pain she'd endured only moments before she flashed. She hated leaving Terran behind, but he would have dragged her back to the fortress, without the answers she so desperately wanted. Everything had happened so fast. She thought of the girls she left behind in the salon she thought she owned. Her mortal life. They wouldn't know her now. She felt a twinge of sadness. She had to leave that life, forever.

Payton trudged along, trying to keep a steady pace and stay alert at the same time. It was quiet in the woods. She was beginning to realize it was a little too quiet when she heard a twig snap. She turned toward the sound.

"Hello," said a stranger with a large grin on his face.

Payton stepped back.

"Who are you?" She asked, trying not to sound scared out of her wits. "Are you following me? Why are you following me?"

"Don't be afraid," the stranger replied, "you are on my land. I saw you from a distance and decided to investigate. You are trespassing. Who are you?" He asked.

She glared at the stranger now standing only a few feet away from her. He was a striking figure. Tall, blonde, and hot! 'Oh crap!' She thought. 'Stop it. Payton Just stop it! You're married, remember?' She stared, he was almost god-like. Her eyes widened as the thoughts entered her mind. 'God-like!' She stepped back a few more paces.

"I asked you first," she said. "Who are you?"

"Ah, where are my manners? I am Aurel." He answered, then asked "And you are?

"Payton."

"Very nice to meet you, Payton." Aurel said, then bowing slightly.

Chapter 27

Aurel walked around Payton slowly, examining her closely. At first, puzzled, wondering who this person was. She looked different; no aura, she smelled different; curious. He had never had any problem figuring out a mortal before. No fear either, really, she is cautious though. Curious.

Payton was watching Aurel very closely also. Who is this? Looks like he could be a god, yet his name was not familiar to her. Maybe he was a god in another realm. He seemed different.

"So," Payton started. "Um, so where are you from and why were you watching me?"

"I live here." Aurel answered.

"In this forest?" she asked.

"In this land." Aurel said.

"You could be more specific … Aurel." Payton said, annoyance now apparent in her voice.

"This is my homeland – Romania. I live here." He said, then asked, "And yourself? What brings you here?"

"Um … I'm looking for someone." Payton answered.

"May I be of some assistance?" he offered.

"Why? I don't know you, we just met and you're offering to help? Okay, buddy, what's going on here?" She questioned again.

"You are very suspicious, woman," he said. "There is nothing 'going on.' I thought I might point you in the right direction, if I can."

"Oh." She blushed a bit. "Sorry."

"Very defensive, I must say. But it is a good character to have in these lands. One must defend one's self, especially … a woman." He said, a slight grin appearing.

"Fine," she retorted, "this 'woman' is looking for …," she broke off. Why the hell should she ask a total stranger where the Anords could be? If they're hiding out in Romania, around the Carpathians, they are a long way from home. She was getting lost in her thoughts, her suspicions …

"Payton?"

She blinked. "I don't think you can help, but thank you." She said and started to walk on.

"Perhaps I can help." He said, following her. "I've lived here for many years. I know the land. All of it."

Payton thought for a moment, then said, "okay. So, say I let you help me. How do I know I can trust you?"

"You do not know," he answered, "but, I'm sure you trust your instincts. What do they tell you?"

"If I go on that," she said, "I'd have to say … you aren't a threat to me, but, there is something about you that's not – for lack of a better word – normal."

Aurel laughed. It was a genuine laugh. Not menacing.

"Perhaps we will figure each other out as we travel along." He said.

They both walked along a path Payton found. It looked well-travelled. It was a beautiful forest. She could really lose herself here. No worries, leave things behind her for a while. Why did she have to be a god? So called 'Chosen.' Argh! So much had been dumped on her shoulders in such a short time. She was trying so hard to get some answers and hoping to find them here. They walked for some time before Aurel spoke, "May I ask, what you are looking for Payton?"

"It's 'who' actually." She said.

"Alright, who?"

She continued "Her name is Lilith. From what I can deduce, she must be here somewhere. My gut tells me she's in the mountains. She's with …," Payton didn't want to say Lilith was with the 'evil' gods of her realm and … oh man. "There's some group, sect, whatever you'd call it, called the Anords. I'm sure I'll find her there."

Aurel stopped. Anords. He had heard of them. He had heard gossip from some of the old people in the villages around the country. He thought it was just that – gossip. Payton turned around. Aurel was several feet behind her, not following as before.

"Something wrong?" she asked.

Aurel said, "These Anords – they are real?" Payton nodded.

"I have heard the old people of the villages talk of them I thought it was idle gossip, and did not pay any attention to it. But, the villagers, they seem afraid. They do not venture far from home. They are afraid."

"Have you seen them?" Payton asked.

"I cannot say that I have," he answered, "but I have seen unusual activity in the mountains recently. It seems there were more storms and very bright lightening; more than I have ever known. Perhaps, your Anords?"

"They are not 'My Anords' Aurel, but I am looking for a woman I believe is with them. Her name is Lilith," she said.

"This is intriguing," said Aurel, "now you must follow me instead. I believe I can show you where the storms and lightening were coming from."

"Okay." Payton replied.

Aurel went ahead of Payton, his walk was very graceful. Almost as if he floated.

Flash!

Terran examined the landscape. Romania, he knew it. He looked up at the majestic mountains. He saw the storms brewing and the bright lightening. They were brighter than usual. His heart sank, his stomach ached. He knew Payton was on her way toward the storms. He had to find her, had to stop her. She wasn't ready.

Chapter 28

Payton continued to follow Aurel through the forest until they came to the edge of a clearing. Aurel stopped, held his hand up for Payton to stop.

"Someone is here," he whispered.

Payton moved around Aurel slowly to see what he was seeing.

Two people fighting. One was a very large man and the other, a woman. The man looked very familiar. She'd seen him before too, she was sure of it. But where? And the woman – something about seeing her, her chest hurt. Like a sharp pain.

They weren't fighting either. They were sparring. Practicing! Oh no!

"Well, well! Look who we have here!" a voice from behind Payton said. Payton jumped and Aurel merely turned, gracefully to see her.

Lyradis smiled at seeing Payton's reaction.

"Payton, beloved daughter of Liesson and Ardaria." She said. "Trying to sneak up on us? Spy? No matter. You're here. This saves us so much time. So nice of you! But that is your nature isn't it my dear?"

Payton stared at this woman in front of her, mouth slightly open. 'She knows who I am,' she thought. But Payton didn't know her. A small dark aura began to form around Lyradis. A darkness was starting to spread. Even the illusion of small twinkling stars appeared.

"Lyradis." Payton said firmly.

"I see you have regained some of your memories" Lyradis replied.

"Aurel, run!" Payton shouted.

Aurel seemed to disappear right in front of her. Payton started to run through the dense forest, trying to out-run the darkness she knew was behind her, closing in.

"Orkat!"

Payton heard the shout for him from Lyradis. Orkat! No! She had to get away, to hide and give herself a minute to think of her next move. The villagers were right about the storms, the lightning. What they didn't know is that it was a god, an Anord, who was responsible for it. And there it was, a storm brewing, and a big one! Bright flashes of lightning lit up the sky. With the darkness behind her, the mix of the forces would make it difficult for her to find her way. That was the idea, she knew. She could flash, but that would weaken her once again. She couldn't take that chance. She continued to run, every few yards, zigzagging, trying to get away. From out of nowhere, someone grabbed her hand and turned her in a different direction. It was so fast; she hardly knew what was happening.

When they stopped, Payton looked up to see Aurel, still holding her hand, looking down at her.

"I saw that you were in danger," he said, "and perhaps you needed my help."

"Yeah" Payton said, still panting from her desperate run to getaway. "Thanks."

"Come on," she said, "we have to go, get away."

"Calm yourself Payton," Aurel soothed. "Look, you are far away from your foes."

Payton followed Aurel's gaze to see that they were at least half a mile away from the darkness and storms.

"How did you do that?" she asked.

"I am … fast," he answered.

"These Anords, that was them?" he asked. Payton nodded. "Only two of them."

"There are more?" Aurel asked.

"Yes." Payton answered. "There are ten more."

"And they are all after you?" His questions kept coming. "Why? You are important to them? That woman – she knew you and your parents?"

"Yes, yes," she said. "Man, I thought I had questions. Yes, she knows who I am, and I now know who she is from what I've been told and from what I've read, and no, before you ask, I don't really know why they're after me." They stood in silence for a few seconds. Payton could see that Aurel was contemplating what to do next.

"We should go," Payton said, and started walking. She had not taken three steps when she heard, "Go where? My dear."

She spun around. Aurel was on his knees, agony in his face. A gold vine, with thorns was wrapped around his neck.

"Aurel!" She shouted and reached back for him. She felt a large hand grab her arm, holding her back. Vladok.

Payton tried to struggle. It was no use.

She saw them appear one by one. The Anords. All of them. Twelve gods of chaos. She looked down at Aurel again; he vanished. What? What the hell! How did he get out of that?

"Well, well," Lis spoke up. "We have another immortal to deal with, don't we? Krerok, Ulgor, scan the area. Find him!" She ordered. Krerok and Ulgor vanished.

Ten Anords left. 'I've got to get away,' Payton thought. She scanned the ten left, encircling her, taking in the appearance of each god to her memory.

"So, this is the famous Payton." Payton heard a voice. Her voice. But she wasn't speaking. Then she saw her coming toward Payton. Can't be! Payton was looking at herself. It was like looking in a mirror.

"Let me introduce myself. Since I know who you are, you should know me. I am Lilith," she said. Lilith smiled sweetly. Payton could see her eyes. They were green, not blue like her own. She could see the evil.

Chapter 29

Terran moved quickly down the path. It was the same path Payton was on, he was sure of it. No sign of her.

Such a beautiful land, he thought. Too bad he couldn't enjoy it. He longed for the days before the battle when Payton was beside him, enjoying each other, happy. Now why did you have to fall in love with a woman, destined to be the most powerful god in the world?' He asked himself. He smiled. How could he not? It was Payton, and he loved her more than life itself. He was a half-breed. She could have chosen anyone. A son of gods. A full god. She chose Terran, knowing he was half mortal. The thought of Payton made him smile, if only for a moment. He continued on – he had to find her. He could almost smell her scent. Wait, that was her scent. Terran stopped. Saw a figure on the ground several yards away. He raced toward it. Payton! Wait! This wasn't Payton. It was a man. He has a vine of thorns around his neck! How? Terran kneeled beside him.

"Please … I beg you … help me," the man gasped.

"Okay, okay" Terran said. He pulled out the leather gloves his father had given him. Being half mortal, he could not touch the vine with bare hands. With gloves on, he could. He carefully un-wrapped the vine from the man's neck. It left behind bloody puncture wounds that were already healing rapidly. The vine now clear from the man's neck, Terran carefully wound it up and put it in a leather pouch.

"Thank you," the man said.

"No problem," Terran said, then asked, "How did you wind up with the vine of thorns around your neck? How are you still alive? That thing is fatal to mortals."

"I am not mortal, sir," he answered. "I was helping a young woman find her way and came upon others. I am Aurel."

Terran helped Aurel to his feet. 'Helping a woman find her way.' Terran thought.

"This woman you were helping, was her name Payton?" Terran asked.

"Yes" Aurel answered.

"What happened? Where is she?" Terran asked, the panic starting to rise in him.

"These Anords, they have her" Aurel said.

The Anords! Damn! He should have kept a better eye on her. What will the Anords do? They might try to kill her. No. They can't. It would kill Lilith too. They would never take that chance. But they may try to keep her, imprison her for eternity. It can't happen.

"Tell me what happened, Aurel," said Terran.

"Don't have time for you – I must try to help Payton," Aurel said, now fully recovered. Aurel turned and started toward the direction he last saw Payton.

Terran followed, "Aurel! Stop!"

Aurel stopped, turned to face Terran. “Sir, I thank you for your assistance, but I must go.” Aurel said.

“No, please,” Terran was pleading. “Payton, I must find her – Please!”

Aurel looked at Terran’s face. It was sad, frightened, and frantic.

“What would you want with her, sir?” he asked.

“She’s … she’s my wife.” Terran answered.

Aurel said nothing. The one woman he had met in many years and she was married. Great!

“Will you tell me what happened?” Terran asked.

Aurel let out a sigh. “Follow me. I will tell you as we go.”

They walked quickly along, although not as quickly as Aurel would have liked. He had to slow down so the mortal could keep up. Aurel told Terran the full account of things from his meeting with Payton until her capture by the Anords, and finally when Terran found him.

“The vine around your neck would have killed a mortal.” Terran said. “You mentioned you were immortal – a god maybe? But from what realm? I’ve never seen you before, and I thought I had met all the gods.”

“I am not a god,” Aurel said. “I am different. I am between worlds, you might say. It is a long story. I just am. Perhaps one day, we will have time for me to tell you. But not now. We are here.”

Terran looked around. Nothing. According to Aurel, this was the spot Payton was when the Anords surrounded her.

"Unfortunately, I could not help her," Aurel whispered. "That vine, I've never experienced that before. There is very little in this world that can harm me. That vine …"

"Yes, well, you are now dealing with a very different world," Terran said. "The world of gods, good and bad. Your first encounter was with the bad. The Anords are a nasty bunch."

"Perhaps I may still help?" Aurel asked.

"There are things you can do, I'm sure, that I can't. Right now, I have a feeling I'll need all the help I can get." Terran answered.

Chapter 30

The fortress was huge. Ugly. There was an air of evil, despair, darkness. It was built into the cliffs of the Carpathians. No towers, no shiny glints of gold sparkling in the sunlight. In fact, there was no sunlight – just clouds, wind and constant drizzle of rain. Miserable. That's what they were about, the Anords, pure misery.

Orkat pushed Payton down the steps to the large double doors, the entry to the fortress. The rest followed in a line. Payton looked back. They had this look on their faces … smug. All of them.

'The arrogance.' Payton thought. The pain around her wrists was hard to endure. She was adamant. She wasn't going to let them win. She was Payton, destined to be all powerful. 'They won't break me.' She learned quickly that to resist the vine of thorns only made the vine tighter. Orkat enjoyed seeing her wince at every tug. They opened the doors. Orkat pushed Payton through.

"Put her in the deepest, darkest cell we have Orkat." Dichune ordered.

Orkat's smile widened. "With pleasure Dichune!" He said, and once again, pushed Payton forward. She stumbled, almost fell, but retained her composure. Lilith ran up to Orkat.

"Wait!" She shouted. "I want to talk to her."

Orkat stopped pulling the end of the vine to make Payton stop. She winced. The vine tightened its grip slightly. Enough to shoot pain through her hands again. Payton felt herself weaken with every jolt of pain. She needed to rest. Regain her strength.

Lilith came up behind Orkat and stopped just inches in front of Payton.

"You will tell me all I need to know," Lilith whispered. "I want answers, and," Lilith was getting closer to Payton ...

"Lilith, stop!" Dichune shouted. "You must not touch her! Not yet!"

Lilith stepped back, the anger rising in her.

"Why the hell not? I can make her cooperate. I know I can." She yelled back at Dichune. "I will have what's mine!"

"Calm yourself my dear," Dichune said. "All in good time. We must do this right or it will not work at all."

"Fine" Lilith huffed.

Payton was grateful for Dichune's interference. She did not have the strength to deal with Lilith right now.

Orkat pushed her toward a small door at the far end of the entrance hall. He opened it and pushed her through. Steps. A spiral of stone steps, seemingly endless. Payton started down the steps, occasionally stumbling. She heard Orkat's snicker every time she stumbled. Finally, the last step.

Ahead was a long hallway, cells lining both sides. They were small cells with thick rot-iron bars for doors. The bars were all intertwined with the vine. At the end of the hallway of cells was a larger one. Payton knew in her mind, it was meant for her. Orkat yanked the vine again. Payton fell to her knees. He walked around her, opened the vine-covered door, and shoved her in. She fell, face in the dirt. Orkat removed the vines from her wrists, backed out and slammed the cell door shut.

Payton lay on the dirt floor, not moving for hours. She was exhausted. She didn't have the energy to move. The sores around her wrists were just starting to heal. She could still feel the sting of those thorns.

She pushed herself up, slowly. It was cold in the cell. She moved toward the cell bars wanting to grab them, shake them. The vines. She couldn't do it. Instead, she turned toward the stone wall. Feeling her way in the darkness, her knee bumped a hard object. She felt it with her hands. It was another stone bench.

Payton didn't care. She just wanted to sit and rest. She could vaguely see some of the stone and dirt on the wall opposite of her. Slowly, her eyes adjusted. It was just that; a deep, dark cave. Cold, damp, and filthy. She thought she could hear rats scurrying around. Great!

She heard a noise from the far end of the hall. Voices! They're coming back – she thought. She didn't bother to look as Orkat and Lyradis approached the cell.

"Get up!" Orkat ordered.

“Now, now, Orkat,” Lyradis said. “We must be more gentle with her.

Orkat sneered. Lyradis turned toward Payton, “Come Payton, and don’t bother to fight us. You are not strong enough. If you cooperate, you will remain unharmed.” ‘For now’ Lyradis thought.

Chapter 31

Aronon rushed into the meeting room, frantic and out of breath.

"Liesson!" he shouted.

Liesson ran to him. "What is it Aronon?" He asked.

"Payton," Aronon gasped, "they have Payton!" Ardaria approached him. "Aronon, you're sure of this?" She asked, her voice filled with fear. He nodded.

"Terran," he continued, "he's told me Payton flashed before he could stop her. He followed as fast as he could, but was too late. He ran into Aurel. Aurel told Terran what happened and now they're both going after her. Alone!"

"We have to help them, Liesson," Ardaria said.

"We don't have time," Liesson replied. "The battle is soon upon us and we cannot spare any of the others. We need all thirteen of us."

"Liesson!" Ardaria yelled. "We must!"

"No!" He shouted.

Ardaria's heart sank. Payton, she couldn't just leave her alone with them. Terran and Aurel are not enough against the Anords. Tears were welling up in her eyes.

Liesson put his arms around Ardaria and hugged her tightly.

"Don't worry Ardaria," he said, "they will not harm her; they can't at this point. They will, however, bring her to the battle. Of this, I am sure."

Liesson turned his attention to the rest of the gods gathered around them.

"Know this!" he spoke loudly. "The Anords will attempt to use Payton as a distraction. Don't let them. Be alert. Be vigilant and be victorious. When any of us have the opportunity to rescue Payton, take it."

All agreed to Liesson's plan, and headed for the exit.

Aronon took Elrani's hand. She gripped it tightly. They followed the others; Liesson and Ardaria the last in line.

Liesson's thoughts moved to Aurel. Why would he bother to get involved? He was an immortal, yes, but not a god. Aurel wasn't one to take sides. Aurel only did what 'Aurel' wanted. He was neither good nor evil. Always neutral. Curious.

All the Guardians were gathered in front of their fortress. All armed. All ready for battle.

Liesson spoke again. "Remember the battle of Trinity. One god lost. Yet to be replaced. The Anords are drunk with the thought of absolute power. We must not let them win. Human kind will depend on it; on us.

Chapter 32

On the battlefield of Trinity, again, Liesson scanned the area. He was the first to arrive. Then the flashes. Guardians, one-by-one, were arriving. As the last guardian was in place, and … flash in the distance. Anords. They're here. Liesson watched as the last Anord flashed in. Dichune. Liesson stepped forward to meet Dichune in the centre of the field.

"Ah, the mighty Liesson," Dichune said as he met up with him.

"Dichune," Liesson replied.

"Slayer of Koris," Dichune continued. "Today it will be you who dies."

"Dichune, we don't have to do this," Liesson said. "We could be as we were, in harmony, equals. Restore balance."

"How can we be in harmony when we are one short Liesson? We are not balanced. You've seen to that." Dichune said.

"There is a way." Liesson argued. "You know this, and yet you resist. Why?"

"You think your lovely daughter can restore all in the universe?" Dichune laughed. "I think we should see what she thinks, shall we?" Dichune waved. Flash!

Two rot-iron cages appeared; large cages with vines wrapped all around them. Through the vines, Liesson could see Payton.

Her hands bound by the same vine of thorns. In the other cage, Lilith. Liesson knew it. Lilith wouldn't be a threat to the Anords. She was evil – pure evil.

Dichune then said, "I am keeping Lilith in a cage for now. She has a great yearn to touch Payton. We both know we can't let that happen."

"You cannot change fate." Liesson growled.

"But Liesson, I think I can. You see, we are gods; we decide fate and if we can control fate in the human world, we can in our world." Dichune said. "Enough talk – Anords!"

The Anords attacked. The Guardians met them in full force. God against God. Payton watched helplessly. She saw the blades flying through the air, each god using their own power to try to gain the advantage over their opponent. She could see the cuts, the bruises on both sides. They healed quickly.

Payton needed to get out. She struggled against the vine holding her. They tightened. It didn't matter. She managed to reach the small knife in her boot. She drew it out, flipped it over and started slicing at the vine. It was working. She could feel it loosen. The vine fell from her wrists. Payton stood in the cage. The fighting was worse. She could see her father face-to-face with Vladok, Liesson wielding his sword, swinging at Vladok. Vladok threw a small silver object that met the blade. Explosion. Payton's eyes grew wider. No! Liesson was ready for it. He saw the silver come and brought up his shield to protect himself. Just in time too. Vladok threw another straight at the shield. Another explosion. Liesson stood up, his shield burnt a little, but still intact.

Payton thought ‘I have to do something!’ Her mind racing, ‘but what?’ She was watching her parents and the rest of the Guardians fight for their lives, for hers. Then she saw him – Aronon. What was he doing here? He’s not a god! He hasn’t got a chance! He’ll be killed!

She saw Lyradis approach Aronon from behind. Her darkness was starting to encircle him. Payton knew that within seconds, he’d be dead. She couldn’t let that happen. Lyradis closed in on Aronon. Payton raised her hands and with all her might, thrust them forward. Boom! So loud and so powerful. All the gods – Guardians and Anords, were thrown. Aronon was saved by Elrani, who grabbed his arm as he was flying past her, from the blast.

Terakas, Guardian, god of fire and warmth, was closest to the cages. He flashed to the one cage Payton was in. He grabbed one of the bars, carefully avoiding the thorns. Flash! He was gone. The cage was gone too.

The Anords flashed, all of them, taking the remaining cage with them.

The Guardians were left alone on the battlefield.

“Everyone – back to the fortress” Liesson ordered. In a flash, the field was empty.

Chapter 33

Terran trudged along behind Aurel, still wondering why Aurel wanted to help him, help Payton. Aurel just met Payton. They'd known each other only minutes and yet he's putting himself on the line for her. "Why?" He had to ask.

"Aurel."

"Yes."

"Why are you doing this?" Terran asked.

Aurel knew Terran was fishing for more than he was willing to tell.

"What's in it for you?" Terran asked again.

"I find this Payton … intriguing. She's different from any woman I have ever met before in my years. She compels me." He answered. He knew Terran wouldn't want to hear it. Aurel couldn't help himself. It just came out and he wasn't sorry he'd said it.

Terran was quiet. He knew exactly what Aurel meant. He wants her. He wants my wife! Bastard! There's no way he's laying a hand on her. Terran was seething. Thinking up ways to rid himself of this, this rival. Terran froze.

'Terran?' – It was his father. 'The battle was cut short. We're not sure why, but we've managed to rescue Payton. She's here, at our fortress. Terran – she's home. You must come now. We have to plan.'

'Yes, father.' Terran replied. The vision faded from Terran's mind.

"I have to go." Terran told Aurel. Aurel stopped, turned to face Terran.

"Go where?" He asked.

"Home. I have to go home." My father told me they've rescued her. My Payton is home." Terran answered.

"May I accompany you?" Aurel asked.

"I go on my own." Terran answered.

"Perhaps, I may still be of service to you and the … Guardians." said Aurel. Terran knew what Aurel wanted, but he also knew that Aurel could probably help, in his own way. Terran wasn't going to make it easy for Aurel.

"I go alone." Terran said again. "But, if you can find the Guardian fortress, I will meet you, and introduce you to them. It will be their decision whether you stay or go."

"Understood." Aurel replied, and then asked "Where is this fortress?"

"Northern Ireland." Terran answered. "I trust you can find it on your own." With that, Terran flashed. Aurel was alone.

Aurel smiled. 'I will meet you in Northern Ireland, young Terran.' He thought. 'It will take a little longer, a couple of days or so, but I will see you again. I will see my compelling Payton."

Chapter 34

The Guardians were back at their fortress. They gathered in the courtyard, surrounding the cage.

"Terakas, the vines," Liesson said loudly. With that, Terakas drew his sword and started slicing through the vines. They fell away easily, revealing Payton inside. She stood motionless, her head hung down. Her appearance shocked the gods. Ardaria raced to the cage, grabbed the iron door and ripped it off its hinges. A mother's power was infinite when it came to their children.

Ardaria ran to her. Her arms wrapped around her only child.

"How could they do this to her? Monsters!"

Payton was so dirty; clothes in rags, barely hanging on to her. Her hair was mussed and matted in places.

"Payton," Ardaria's tears were welling up, "are you hurt? What did they do to you?"

Payton slowly wrapped her arms around her mother, "I'm okay mother, really." She answered. "Their accommodations for me were, to say the least, filthy," she tried to laugh.

"Let me have a look at you," her mother tried to lift her daughter's chin.

"Mother … please. I'm so tired. I need to rest. Take me to my room, please." Payton said.

"Ardaria, let our daughter rest." Liesson intervened. "She can fill us in after she's rested." Liesson hugged Payton. He released her, took her by the hand, and started for the entrance back into the fortress.

Flash!

"Payton!" Terran was back. He ran for her, scooped her up in his arms. "Payton, you're safe!" Terran's happiness to see his wife was unmistakable. He kissed her face all over and finally a long, lingering kiss on the lips. Payton smiled slightly. Terran hugged her tightly. "Don't ever leave me again, my love," Terran whispered to her. She could hear his voice crack a little.

"I won't … my love," she whispered back. She smiled half-heartedly.

They walked back inside the fortress, hand-in-hand.

Epilogue

“Dichune, you have taken a great gamble on this plan of yours,” Lyradis said.

“I know,” he replied.

“And how do you know this plan of yours will work?” Asked Siresha, god of disease and despair, “she is unstable, volatile. We don’t know if we can trust her.”

“She is a god,” Dichune replied, “or at least half … whatever. The point is, we have no choice but to put our trust in her, however unstable she may be. We have prepared her the best way we can. Now it is up to her.”

Eleven sets of eyes rested on Dichune. Skeptical glares. Dichune knew they were wary of the plan he devised. Hell he wasn’t sure himself if she could pull it off.

“Look,” Dichune said, “we had to get her near Terran. He is the only one who knows the final code word. If she can fool him into thinking she is the real Payton, we will find out all those bloody code words and the most important one – the one word that must be said to Payton when the time is right.”

“When the planets align in thirty days, at the twelfth hour, we must make it happen. If we fail, we will forever be resigned to working in unison with the Guardians. ‘*Peace and harmony, in balance*.’” Dichune shuttered those horrible words.

"Lilith must succeed. She knows what's at stake."

"In the meantime, what are we to do with our precious cargo in the dungeon? Hmmm?" Lis asked, arms folded, left brow arched.

"Aurel. Lis, find him. Bring him here. I feel he has an attraction for our 'precious.' She compels him, for some reason. Perhaps we can persuade him to help us." Dichune said, a slight smile on his face.

The only one who can reveal the code words to Payton, was the one she loved completely … perhaps Aurel could divert her……………..

Perhaps.

Find me at:

www.cjbolyne.com

www.facebook.com/CJ.Bolyne